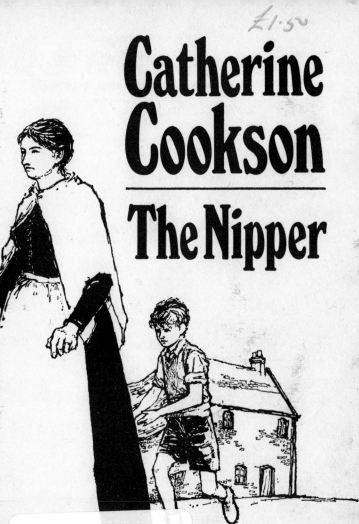

Catherine Cookson

The Nipper

Illustrated by
TESSA JORDAN

MACDONALD AND JANE'S · LONDON

£1.50

Catherine Cookson has also written

JOE AND THE GLADIATOR
MATTY DOOLIN
BLUE BACCY

*To Ross, to help him remember me when he is
very old, around twenty or so*

© Catherine Cookson 1970

First published in Great Britain in 1970
Reprinted in 1974
This impression 1979

Published by
Macdonald and Jane's Publishers Limited
Paulton House
8 Shepherdess Walk
London N1 7LW

ISBN 0 356 03111 X

Printed and bound in Great Britain by
Redwood Burn Limited
Trowbridge & Esher

One

'Boy! Come away from that door and help me with the bundles.'

When the boy didn't move Norah Gillespie stuck her hands on her hips and stared at her son; then she let out a bellow, crying, 'Sandy! Do you hear me?' and he started and turned to her and said, 'Yes, Ma. Yes, Ma.'

She sighed now as he came towards her and when he stood in front of her, her manner changing and her voice soft, she said, 'It's no use, you can't do anything about it,

5

so it will be easier for you if you make up your mind.'

Sandy Gillespie bowed his dark head and hunched his thick shoulders; and when his mother said, 'And another thing you've got to realize: you're no longer a child or even a boy going mad after ponies, you will be sixteen shortly; you're a man, and what you've got to do now is to act like one.'

Sandy's head came slowly upwards, and now there was a look of hurt, of defiance on his face. He knew without being told that he was a man, with a man's responsibilities; he had shouldered a man's responsibilities for two years now. From the day his father had died of the cholera he had worked fourteen hours a day on the farm, not a moan out of him or a grumble; his half-yearly pay of two pounds ten he had tipped up and never asked for a penny back. Still, his mother had always been generous, giving him as much as half-a-crown at times, and with this he had been content, or nearly so, for there was an unrest in him that had nothing to do with money. But the unrest had quietened eighteen months ago when The Nipper had come into his life.

It was on the day he had gone with Farmer Blyth to collect the trees that were needed for supports to bolster the floundering barn. It was in Sir William Stockwell's forest six miles away and the journey itself had been exciting for he had never been more than four miles from the village in his life. When he had reached the forest he had stepped into further excitement for the tree fellers were having sport trying to catch a wild pig. One of them had a gun, which even Sandy knew was against the law, for the man wasn't a keeper. And he was a poor shot into the bargain; instead of killing the pig he shot a young Galloway pony that, in the mêlée, had stampeded, and when they came up to it there it was lying on its side with blood pouring from its neck and a young foal pressed close to its belly and petrified with fear, so much so that it couldn't run.

The tree fellers knew they would be in for trouble if the keepers found the pony, and so they hoisted it up on to a cart to sell later, perhaps to some pie maker in the lower part of Shields, or if not there up in the city of Newcastle. But what to do with the young foal? The head feller was for killing it, but Sandy had sprung forward and, taking the stricken animal in his arms, had gabbled, 'Give it me. Give it me. Let me have it, I'll see to him.'

'Have sense, boy,' Farmer Blyth roared at him; 'ponies grow. Where do you think you're going to keep it? How do you think it's going to eat?' And at this Sandy had said, 'I'll . . . I'll pay for his keep, master; I'll work an extra hour a day for it. And . . . and I'll train it. You could use it for the trap, the little one that's lying behind the barn. It would do for Miss Katie, it would do for her fine.'

Staring at the boy, Farmer Blyth had seen the possibility; but he was a harassed and worried man and the story could have ended there. However, Sandy, the animal lying immobile in his arms, its heart hardly beating, had run some distance before, turning and facing the farmer and the four wood cutters, he cried defiantly, 'I'm going to keep him; if I have to walk away now and scrounge, I'm going to keep him.'

Farmer Blyth had glared at the boy. He was being defied, and what he would have liked to say was, 'Get going then and see how far you get before you starve to death,' but this boy was the only help he had on his farm and, although of no great size, he had stamina and did the work of a man, and longer hours than any farm

hand would do these days without shouting about it. He'd
have to pay a man nine shillings a week for the work
this boy did, or put up with the scum and indifferent
labour from the dole men that the town clerks sent out
to the farms to work off their payment. What was more,
if the boy left the mother would go too, and so he would
lose help in the dairy, in the house, and in the fields. For
a shilling a week and her food and her cottage free,
Norah Gillespie did the work of two women.

All Farmer Blyth could do now was to bluster, 'I'll
have something to say to you when I get back, me boy.
And so will your mother. She'll skin your hide when you
take that in.' He dug a finger towards the now shivering
foal, and Sandy let out a great sigh of relief and held the
animal closer to him. He had won; it was his, this little
nipper.

And that's how The Nipper had come into Sandy's
life. And now on this day, Saturday the twenty-seventh
of June, eighteen hundred and thirty, his whole life seemed
ended, for today he and The Nipper were to be parted.

His mother's voice broke into his agonised thoughts.
'He'll likely get a good home,' she said softly.

A good home! He looked back into her eyes, dark
brown like his own, and he said, 'In the market! And
driven there by Billy Foggerty, who'll put an extra long
nail in the end of his goad 'cos he doesn't like me.'

'No, no, he won't; not with the horses, they're biddable.'

'I've seen him. I've seen him.' He screwed up his face
at her as he gripped his jaw tightly with one hand.

Now his mother was holding him by the shoulders, her
voice harsh again, saying, 'Look, you've got to stop this.
He's goin', and nothin' you can do, or I can do, or anybody else, will stop it. Anyway, when all's said and done
what is the loss of a pony against our home?' She now

8

thrust out her arm and indicated the homely looking room. 'And the master losing his farm and going as a herdsman to somebody else after being his own man all his life. And how do you think the mistress feels having to live in a cottage no bigger than this?' Again she thrust her arm out. 'And Miss Katie, who's been used to a room to herself all her life, now having to sleep in the kitchen in the place where they're going. Two little rooms after a house full of big ones, with pantries, wash-house, dairies, the lot; how do you think they're feeling? An' you going nearly out of your mind 'cos of a dratted Galloway?'

'He's not JUST a Galloway.'

'Don't you raise your voice at me, boy. I say he's a Galloway; he's just one of dozens of the same like about the country.'

When Mrs Gillespie talked of the country she did not envisage the beautiful upper reaches of the River Tyne but rather the land lying between the riverside villages and towns on the south bank and the inland coalfields, which land was dotted with farms, gentlemen's estates and open fell. And she emphasized her limited horizon by saying now, 'Our world is small, boy, but large enough to starve in, and that's what we'll do if you don't pull yourself together. We've got to get all this ready for Bradshaw's cart within the hour, and then we'll be gone. And that's what you've got to face up to ... We'll be gone; we're going one road and The Nipper's going another.'

'Oh, Ma!' There was an expression on Sandy's face as if his mother had struck him and he turned about and dashed out of the door, across the mud-ridged farmyard, dry in patches, puddled in others, past the cow shed, the piggeries and the long barn, and he didn't stop running until he came up against a long pole set in notches at each side of a gap in a low dry-stone wall. He leant over it for a moment, his head on his chest; then slowly raising it, he looked to the far end of the field and whistled softly.

The Galloway lifted its head, turned, paused a moment, and galloped towards him, mud and turf scudding as it came through a marshy patch. Then it was at the bar, its neck pressed hard against it, its lips moving over its teeth as if in wordless greeting, and its soft nose was thrust against his shoulder, once, twice, three times, and Sandy, his voice breaking, muttered, 'I can't, lad. I can't.' But when again his shoulder was nudged he shook his head from side to side, glanced behind him towards the farm buildings and the cottage, where his mother was waiting for his help, and with a swift desperate movement dived under the bar, and gripping the long, glossy brown mane, swung himself up on to the little horse's back, and they were off, galloping round the field, boy and animal as one.

When they came abreast of the gate again the pressure from his knees and a 'Whoa! Nipper' brought the pony to a halt, and he slid from its back and stood for a moment, his head pressed tight against its flank. And now The Nipper turned its head and looked at him, then gave a small neigh, and Sandy stood back and said, 'All right.'

It would be the last time he would ever put his friend through his paces. Holding out his hand as if in greeting and his words cracking in his throat, he said, 'Hello there. How you keepin'?' And The Nipper lifted his right fore-leg and pawed twice. Now Sandy turned and, limping away, said, 'Sore leg. Sore leg,' and The Nipper followed him, giving a good imitation of walking on a damaged hoof.

Turning to him again, Sandy said in a voice that was little above a whisper, 'Down and out. Down and out,' and on this The Nipper lowered himself to the ground, fell on his side, closed his eyes and became inert.

It was too much. As Sandy gazed down on the motionless animal he could see it as the real thing. Perhaps shortly, if no farmer bought him, that was how The Nipper would look lying in the slaughter house; and there was little chance of any farmer buying him with the small farmers all being put out of business, their land being enclosed by the big farmers. And the big farmers hadn't much use for Galloways; they couldn't pull the plough, and they weren't big enough for the ladies' gigs – such as The Nipper were only suitable for little traps like Miss Katie's.

As he bent under the pole to run back towards the farm The Nipper's voice followed him, neighing loudly now in protest because the game hadn't been finished – he was always given a crust after the last trick.

When he reached the yard, Sandy saw Bradshaw's flat cart outside the cottage and, talking to the carrier, Jeff Telford.

Jeff Telford was a drover and in Sandy's opinion a decent man, because unlike Billy Foggerty he didn't take pleasure in the pain of animals.

When he approached them, Jeff Telford turned to him and said, 'Hello there, lad,' and Sandy replied briefly, 'Hello.' Although Jeff Telford was the lesser of two evils, he was still an evil.

The carrier now said, 'Well, come on; let's get your stuff loaded and away.' And on this he disappeared into the cottage while Jeff Telford went towards the farmhouse. Disregarding his mother's voice, Sandy quickly followed the drover and in a hurried whisper said, 'Jeff, will . . . will you tell me where he goes, The Nipper?' He jerked his head in the direction of the field, explaining further, 'The young Galloway.'

Jeff Telford glanced back towards the cottage and muttered, 'I've just promised your mother I'll keep mum; an' it would be better like that.'

'Aw, Jeff, Jeff man; I only want to know where he goes.'

'Well.' Again Jeff glanced towards the cottage, then said quickly, 'You're moving over Hebburn way, aren't you?'

'Aye, Ballast Row; outside the town on the edge of the fell.'

Jeff Telford looked at him sadly, then said, 'Ballast Row. Well, beggars can't be choosers, lad; it'll be a roof until you find somethin' else. Anyway, I'll be around yonder this day week; I'll drop in.'

'Thanks, Jeff.' But now Sandy bit on his lip and he said, 'But what's the use? I'll not be there; we're going with the farm ganger fruit pickin' up Low Fell way. I understand it's a good six or seven miles each journey. Leave at half past four in the mornin' they tell us, and you're lucky if you get back at eight.'

Jeff Telford sighed, then said, 'Well, I can't do no more, lad. The next best thing I can say is, if there's anybody around Ballast Row I'll leave word with them; or, I tell you what.' He stabbed him in the shoulder with his forefinger. 'I'll be driving the cattle from Hursthill Manor on Tuesday of next week. Now I could leave word with the young miss. I'll likely see her about; she's going into the dairy I hear.'

'Yes .. oh aye.' Sandy nodded. 'That's an idea. Thanks, Jeff.'

'Good-bye, lad; and the best of luck.'

As Sandy turned back towards the cottage it came to

him that the only time he would be able to go and see Miss Katie at the Manor farm would be on a Sunday, and that was a whole week ahead.

He met his mother in the doorway. She had her arms spread wide carrying a drawer from the chest, and he saw by her face that she was in a temper, but he also saw that she was trying to suppress it and not vent it on him, for she pushed roughly past him towards the cart without a word.

He went into the cottage and the carter said, 'Lend a hand here, lad,' and he took one end of the chest of drawers. And so the loading went on. The two plank beds, the feather ticks, the trestle table, the high-backed arm-chair and the four wheel-backs; then the assortment of rough crockery, and lastly, the only ornaments in the house, a pair of china greyhounds with rabbits lying at their feet, and the Bible, which neither of them could read.

When the cottage was empty, Norah Gillespie took off her hessian apron, put her black shawl around her shoulders, and, after one long sad look round the room, she went to Sandy, where he was standing near the open door – he, too, taking his silent farewell of the place where he had been born – and she said gently, 'Come, boy; we'll say our good-byes.' And he turned and followed her.

In the yard she said to the carter, 'We'll catch you up; we'll cut over the Fell,' and he answered, 'Right, Missis.'

Side by side they now walked towards the farmhouse, there to see Farmer Blyth coming out of the kitchen door. The farmer was a man in his forties but he appeared old; his shoulders were stooped and his face lined. He stopped and looked at them and said, 'Well, this is it, Norah,' and she answered quietly, 'Yes, Master.'

'Good-bye.' He held out his hand, and she took it but

remained silent. Then he was holding Sandy's hand, clasping it warmly. 'Good-bye, lad,' he said. 'I wish you could have got set-on along of me. But if ever I hear of an opening I'll speak up for you.'

'Thank you, Master.'

'Master!' Farmer Blyth repeated, then closed his eyes. 'No longer, lad. No longer. It's me who'll be mastering from this day on. I never thought I'd live to see it. But there; it's bad for me, but it's worse for the mistress and the young one.'

He turned now and looked towards the kitchen, and there appeared in the doorway Mrs Blyth, her face red and swollen with crying, and by her side a young girl, slight of figure with hair so fair as to be called silver. She wasn't crying, but her grey eyes were wide and moist and her lips were trembling.

'Good-bye, mistress.' Norah Gillespie stood before Mrs Blyth and the farmer's wife said brokenly, 'Oh Norah! Norah, that I should see this day.'

'Good-bye, Miss Katie.'

'Good-bye, Norah.' The young girl's voice was just a whisper. And now she turned her eyes on to Sandy and moved towards him, and it was noticeable that she was slightly crippled, one leg being shorter than the other, her left side being pulled downwards with each step.

Sandy looked into her face, a face that sometimes punctuated his dreams at night; he saw it in the most odd situations, but he was always pleased to see it, for it was a beautiful face.

'Good-bye, Miss Katie.' Sandy's voice was hoarse. He went to proffer his hand, then in embarrassment dropped it to his side again.

Katie's lids were blinking rapidly as she asked, 'Will . . . will you come to see us, Sandy?' and to this he inclined his head once sharply before turning abruptly away.

He was aware that his mother was speaking to him; he took no notice but hurried on, across the farmyard and through the gate on to the rough road, and there, leaning against the outer wall of the barn he stood waiting for her coming, trying all the while to press back the burning sting that was making his eyes water.

When Norah Gillespie came up to him she wagged her head at him, saying, 'Acting like that, never saying goodbye to the mistress.' Yet although her words held a reprimand her tone was soft, soft and broken with her feelings. And now, side by side, they walked up the road, a fifteen year old boy who had to be a man, and his thirty-two year old mother whose shoulders were weighed down with worry.

Two

At four o'clock in the afternoon when they arrived at Ballast Row, Sandy's mind was lifted from his own misery concerning The Nipper by the sight of the place that was to be his future home.

Ballast Row had once consisted of ten cottages; now only the two end ones were standing, the rest were roofless, and strangely the walls of the two middle ones seemed to have sunk some way into the ground.

He stopped on the dusty road and stared at his mother and she, her tone now bitterly defensive, said, 'I couldn't do anything else, it was this or The House, and you didn't want us to land up there, did you? It'll have to do for the time being; it's only a shilling a week.'

'A shilling a week!' Sandy muttered now as his nose wrinkled against the smell that came from the empty dwellings. 'They should pay people to live here.'

'It won't be so bad when we get the place scrubbed out and the walls white-washed.'

'That smell, Ma.'

Norah Gillespie's chin jerked upwards and her eyes blinked rapidly as she muttered, 'It's a filthy lot that live in the end house; they're in the mine, three boys and the father, they live like pigs. But no, that's an insult to the pigs. Anyway, we needn't have anything to do with them.'

The carter was starting to unload the bits and pieces

of furniture and she said to him, 'We'll leave it all out-side until we get the place scrubbed out.'

'Just as you like,' he said, and when he had taken the last pot from the cart she paid him the two shillings agreed on, and as he pocketed the money he shook his head sadly at her, saying, 'I'm sorry to see you come to this, Mrs Gillespie,' to which she answered proudly, 'It won't be for long.'

He looked around, then said, 'Isolated an' all. You'll miss the company.'

'Why did they build a row of cottages out here on the fell land?' asked Sandy now of the carter, and he answered, 'Why, lad, they were for the pit men; the pit's only a mile or so away over yonder.' He pointed. 'But they scattered when the ground gave way above a seam. It often happens; the galleries below fall in—' he kicked his toe into the dusty road – 'and then what's on top just crumbles. Like an earthquake you know. In this case, it went plumb through the middle. Still, you're safe enough in the end house; the ground has been settled for a good few years now, and the Mullens—' he thumbed to the opposite end of the row – 'they usually have the place to themselves 'cos with one thing and another, nobody will live near them.'

Sandy stared at the carter. He knew one of the reasons why people didn't want to live near these Mullens – his nose made that evident enough – and he would have liked to ask what the other reasons were, but his mother was saying now, 'There's no time to waste, there's water to be carried and work to be done.' She nodded at the carter, saying, 'Thanks for your help.' And to this he answered, 'You're welcome, you're welcome'; then turned his horse and left them.

When Sandy followed his mother over the threshold and

into the main room of the cottage he was appalled, not only with the dirt but by the fact that the fireplace wall was cracked in a number of places and that there was an inch wide gap running up by the side of the chimney. As if his mother had been reading his thoughts she snapped at him, 'I know all about it. I know all about it. Mud and straw will soon fix that once we get the place clean. Now stop it!' He stared at her before saying, 'I'm not saying anything, Ma.'

'No, but I know what you're thinkin'.'

'Well, if you do—' he squared his shoulders now and thrust his chin out – 'you'll know that if it rests with me we won't be paying many weeks' rent here.'

Her voice suddenly dropping and her head drooping with it she said, 'I'm with you there lad'; and on this he walked to her and with an unusual expression of affection, for what they felt for each other was rarely expressed in outward form, he put his hand on her shoulder and said, 'I'm sorry. Don't worry, I'll find a way out.'

Her eyes moist, she turned quickly away from him, saying, 'There's a burn about five minutes' walk away and a good spring above it; we'll have water, that's something, but—' she walked to the door and looked up and down the deserted street and her tone changing, she said, 'You'd think by the look of things that the people hereabouts had never seen water in their lives. Here.' She stooped and handed him two wooden buckets; then pointing across the open land to where it rose to form a hill about a hundred yards away, she said, 'Just beyond there you'll come to it. Now look slippy! ...'

Sandy looked slippy eight times within the next three hours and the shadows were lengthening and the twilight beginning by the time they had moved the furniture into the house and got the fire going and the kettle boiling.

When at last they sat down at the table and his mother cut four thick slices of rye bread on which she spread pig fat before pushing them across to him he felt too tired to eat, until she urged him gently, 'Eat your bite, boy, then we'll get to bed early and have a long day the morrow putting things to rights.' She glanced towards the crack in the wall through which they could see the fading light.

It was as they were unrolling the feather ticks with which to cover the wooden bases that served as beds that they heard the commotion outside.

After one glance at his mother, Sandy went to the door and opened it, and there, standing facing him were three boys; one about as tall as himself, one a good deal shorter and a third one looking little more than a child. They were black from head to foot; only their lips, where their tongues kept licking, and their eyes showed any colour. It was the middle one who spoke first. 'You gonna live here?' he said in a thick rough sounding voice.

'Yes.' Sandy nodded at them.

'Huh!' The two younger ones looked at each other and laughed, and it was the taller of the two who spoke again. 'Me da won't like that . . . me da's Big Mullen.'

Sandy was about to retort, 'Well, if he doesn't like it he can lump it, can't he?' but he warned himself to go careful, and so he said, 'We're paying rent, we've a right here.'

'Oh aye.' It was the youngest one speaking now. 'Wait till you see me da; he'll make ya change your mind..' his voice trailed away and Sandy saw them now lift their eyes as one to his mother, who had come to the door, and he watched their mouths drop into gapes.

'Hello,' said Norah Gillespie kindly; but not one of them answered, they just continued to stare. Perhaps, Sandy thought, it was the cleanness of her, or her face that looked bonny, but whatever it was she had silenced their tongues, and they moved away backwards still staring.

Sandy closed the door, wondering as he did so about one thing; the biggest boy hadn't opened his mouth . . .

It seemed only a short time later when Sandy was brought wide awake and upright out of a wonderful dream, in which he was galloping around the field on The Nipper, by someone battering on the door and the sound of oaths filling the night air.

His mother's voice came to him through the darkness, whispering, 'Don't get up.' But when the drunken roaring became louder he heard her rise from the bed and move towards the door, and then, her voice almost drowning that of the man outside, she yelled, 'I'll give you a minute to get yourself away and into your house, and if I hear another word out of you after that, I'll give you the contents of the kale pot, and it's just on the boil.'

There followed a silence as heavy and as thick as the blackness. Then this was broken by a loud, drunken laugh and the voice saying, 'Come on out and let me have a decko at ya.' And Norah Gillespie answered, 'The minute's nearly up, and I warned you, mind.'

Again the laugh came and again the silence, but the next thing they heard was the voice coming from a distance now, singing loudly.

Sandy heard his mother groping her way back to her bed, and sleep gone from him, he lay thinking that all the Mullens were going to be problems, and that the father would pose the biggest one . . .

He awoke with his mother's hand on his shoulder; it was day and she was smiling down on him, saying, 'Have this drop of tea,' and he pulled himself up and smiled back at her, saying 'Oh, ta!' As he took the mug from her he looked round the room and blinked, and it returned to him in a painful rush where he was.

As he sipped at the hot tea it also came to him that in a short while he would have to confront the man called Big Mullen, and more than likely be knocked on to his back if he opened his mouth. But that wouldn't stop him putting up a fight if the fellow got at his ma ... Yet remembering last night, he thought that his ma's tongue might have more effect than his own fists ...

Half-an-hour later Sandy unbolted the front door and stood looking out on to the fells. Everything looked clean and bright; the sun was warm, the sky was high, but there was a terrible stench from the ruined houses to the left of him. The animals on the farm never smelt like this; he would have been ashamed to let the pig sty get into this state. He turned and looked at his mother who was taking off her hessian apron and smoothing her hair back. He watched her pick up her black shawl from the top of the chest and put it over her head as if she was going on a visit, as indeed she was. As she came to the door she said with a half smile, 'When your da was dealin' with an unruly bull he always said look it in the eye, poke it in the chest, and bawl your head off ... Come on.'

They walked side by side past the eight houses, holes gaping in the walls where the window frames had been, all of their doors missing and everything resembling wood stripped away, and when they came to the end house Sandy touched her arm and whispered, 'Look, Ma, let me deal with him ... I can hold me own.' And she smiled at him tenderly and proudly as she said, 'I know you can, lad; but there's more ways of killing a cat than drowning it. We'll try my way first.'

Her way brought Sandy's eyes wide when she took her fist and hammered on the door. When there was no response to her first hammering she repeated the process, louder this time; and now there came a series of grunts and mutterings and a loud oath followed by a command, and when the door opened and the eldest boy stood there blinking in the strong sunlight Norah Gillespie went straight into battle. 'Is your da not up yet?' she demanded. 'Eight o'clock on a Sunday morning!'

The boy gaped at her, glanced back into the room, then looked at her again as she went on, 'He wanted to have a decko at me. Well I'm here; where is he?'

There was dead silence in the room behind the boy, then two small figures appeared standing in short, ragged and dirty shirts. They too stared up at her, and in more surprise than they had done yesterday they stared as if they were looking on an apparition. Now there came a movement behind them and a man pushed the boys aside and stood blinking in the strong sunlight.

Sandy's first impression of Big Mullen made him want to burst out laughing, for Big Mullen was hardly any taller than himself, nor had he any width. It was only when he said, 'What the hell!' that Sandy realised how he came by his name, for his voice was deep and thick and gave the impression of power.

'I'll thank you to mind your language, drunk or sober. You woke me out of me sleep last night. You wanted to see me. Well, here I am.'

Sandy looked from his mother to the peering, blinking man and his muscles tensed and his own fists clenched for he fully expected the man's fists to come out at her. He had seen men like this before, ignorant uncouth men whose only answer to a woman when she stood up for herself was a blow. But Big Mullen just continued to stare at his mother, and Sandy looked from him to her. He saw that the shawl had fallen back from her head, and her bright brown hair was gleaming, and two curly bits had escaped from the tight bun at the back of her head and were dangling on her cheek.

When Big Mullen now said slowly, 'Why didn't your man come?' he watched her hitch the shawl back on to her head; then she said stiffly, 'My man is passed on; this is my man now.'

When she put her hand on his arm Sandy wished he were taller and broader, but he met the eyes of Big Mullen, and unflinching he held his gaze until his mother's voice broke in again, saying, 'We're not for stayin' here long, but as long as we do I want to be left in peace, you and your brood at one end, and us at t'other. An' I'll thank you to get some of the filth cleared up.' She thumbed towards the derelict houses. 'You're askin' for a fever if this heat keeps up.'

There followed a short silence; then she nodded briefly at him and said, 'Good-day to you,' and as one, she and Sandy turned away and walked along the Row, knowing that four pairs of eyes were on them. But no word of abuse was flung at them.

When they entered the cottage again Sandy closed the door and, leaning against it, he put his head back and quietly began to chuckle. And the chuckle grew into a spasm of agonising laughter until he had to throw himself face downwards on to the bed and smother it in case it reached the Mullens at the other end of the street, and all the while his mother stood over him, saying, 'Ssh! Stop it now, boy.' Yet she, too, was laughing; but when at last he rolled over and looked at her his face was wet and sober looking.

Rubbing at his cheeks, he got up from the bed and

said, 'I'll make the mud to clag the crack; then I'll dig a midden at the bottom of the yard,' and his mother answered, 'Do that. Aye, do that.' Then she added on a deep laugh, 'Did you see the look on his face?'

It was in the early afternoon that Sandy, after a dinner of pea soup and rye bread, said, 'I'm going out for a while,' and his mother turned sharply to him and asked, 'Where?' Her eyes dropped to the bulge in his pocket as she spoke, and then she added quickly, 'Be careful now. Anyway it isn't a good time; you know they come in from the towns on a Sunday rabbit snaring. But whatever you do don't go on anybody's land.'

'All right, Ma.' The sharp movement of his head seemed to add, 'I've heard all that afore,' and her voice raised now, she cried at him, 'What you've got to remember is that wherever you go nowadays you're on somebody's land.'

'Not on the fells, Ma,' he said patiently; 'it's common land, you know it is.'

'Common land, huh!' she said. 'And the gentry enclosing it in lumps every week. We've got common land no more, lad, so I'm tellin' you, go careful.'

'All right, Ma; don't worry.' He nodded at her, then went out, glad to get away from Ballast Row for a while.

Out on the fells the air was clean, the distant hills showed warm brown though they would shortly turn to mauve and purple with carpets of new heather.

He told himself he'd make for the hills in the far distance. He could just see a sloping copse with mounds and hillocks at its foot; that was where the rabbits would be.

The distance to the copse was much longer than he had gauged, almost a mile, but when he reached it, he was rewarded by the evidence that there were lots of rabbits about. Some of the mounds were dotted with their holes. He took the wire from his pocket, prepared his rude snare, and placed it at the entrance to a hole; then carefully retreating, taking the lead wire with him, he lay down behind the cover of an outcrop of rock and, his finger held trigger-wise through the end loop of wire, he waited.

After twenty minutes lying thus his arm was in a cramp and his fingers were stiffening, and he was wondering humorously whether the rabbits were all having a nap or had gone out visiting when he was startled, not by a tug on the wire, but by a cry, a protesting cry that ended in a whimper, and he looked quickly up to the copse on the hill behind, then towards the land to the right of him where there were more hillocks, then to the left where the land dipped away; and when the cry came again he knew it was from that direction. Reluctantly he withdrew his finger from the wire and got to his feet, and very cautiously, his body bent now and taking shelter behind the boulders as he went, he approached the ridge of land from which the valley dropped.

His cautiousness was inbred, for a cry such as he had heard could mean a fight, possibly between the Irish and the miners because the miners hated the Irish, as did any unemployed farmworker, for it was the Irish who came over in their boat loads to work for less money, and not only to take men's jobs but their homes. There were fights almost to the death with the Irish, and so his head came cautiously above the mound. But what he saw wasn't a fight between the Irish and the miners, but a one-sided battle between two small miners and an old man.

From his position he was looking down into a cul-de-sac in the hillside and at the far end in a clump of bracken lay an old man, peculiar for three things. He had a tremendous amount of hair not only hanging down in a beard but also down his back, and one leg was cut off below the knee, and one of his hands was a hook. What was more, he was protecting himself from pieces of flying rock.

Sandy's eyes now flashed to the point from which the missiles were being thrown, and there were the two youngest Mullens, their faces impish, hurling the stones every time the old man tried to rise.

Sandy didn't stop to think. Still bent low, he made his way swiftly along the side of the ridge; then darting between boulders he came up from behind the two boys and, grabbing their shoulders, startled them in their devilish play.

'What d'you think you're up to?' He twisted them round, and they looked comical in their surprise and in the fact that they had been washed, after a fashion, for their ears were still black rimmed, as were their eyes. He was seeing them clearly for the first time. He said again, 'What d'you think you're up to?'

'Havin' a game,' the younger one muttered. 'It's only Mad Mark. He was asleep; we pinched his crutch.'

Sandy looked to where the boy was pointing and saw a home-made crutch; and now he glowered at them, crying, 'For two pins I'd belt you with it.'

'You lay a finger on us an' me da'll rip you up.'

'I'm not afraid of your da or anybody else, an' you can tell him that.' His anger was making him brave, and now he thrust them from him, crying, 'Sling your hook while you're able. Go on!' And they scampered away, their bare feet seeming not to feel the sharp-edged shale that covered the path.

Now Sandy picked up the crutch and, his own bare

feet slithering on the grass, he reached the bottom of the hollow and made his way to the old man. Within a few feet of him he stopped and, laying the crutch on the ground, pushed it towards him, saying, 'They've gone; you'll be all right now.'

He was looking into two pale bright eyes which were staring at him from the tangle of grey and white hair, and when the man did not make any comment, he said, 'Are you hurt?'

For answer the old man grabbed at the crutch and lumbered up on to his foot, but still he did not speak, he just stared at Sandy, and Sandy, now embarrassed, began a fumbling explanation on his own. 'I...I was rabbitin' up yonder.' He pointed to the top of the hill. 'I heard them.' He did not say he had heard the old man's cry. 'They're young devils. We've come to live next to them, an' goin' to have trouble I think. Well.' He now backed two steps from the silent weird figure, saying, 'Have to see about a rabbit. They're...they're wide awake the day, not havin' any. So long.' He backed another two steps before turning about and climbing out of the hollow.

When he was on the ridge he looked down and to his amazement there was no sign of the old man. He looked about him. It was as if he had flown away. To get up yon side of the hollow he'd have to be going like a young hill-climber, and he was an old man with one leg and a crutch, aye, and only one hand. He shook his head, then made his way back among the boulders and took up his position once more with his finger through the wire.

Within the next hour he set his trap in three different places without a rabbit even coming within yards of it.

He was lying now behind a mound and was just about

to get to his feet and give it up as a bad job when something heavy came out of the air above him, hit him on the shoulder, then fell in front of his knees.

He had cried out in surprise. And now with his hand across his mouth he stared down at the fine hare lying on the ground; then quickly he looked upwards to the top of the high boulder but he could see no one.

Scrambling to his feet he ran round the boulder but there he was confronted by a wall of rock rising from the ground not six feet away and this merged into the hillside further up and became covered in brush. There was no movement, nothing.

He came back and picked up the hare. He had never seen a bigger or fatter one. He looked upwards towards the hill again and now, his face bright, he cupped his mouth with his hands and shouted, 'Ta! Ta! Thanks!' Then rolling up his wire and thrusting it into his pocket, he pushed the hare up under his coat and ran for home.

'I tell you, Ma, that's how it happened; it came out of thin air. It was the old fellow, I know it was.'

'What did you say the boys called him?'

'Mad Mark.'

She nodded at him now. 'That rings a bell. There's an old fellow lives in the hills, I heard tell of him years ago, but he was just like a bogey man, you know.' She nodded, her face spreading into a smile. 'Me mother used to say, "You behave yourself or else I'll pack you off to Mad Mark," but that's many years ago.'

'He's very old, I should say sixty.'

'Oh, he'll be more than that, more than that.'

'Well, he could be; you can't really tell.'

She looked at the hare and stroked its silky skin; then looking at Sandy again she exclaimed softly, 'It's strange where you meet up with friends,' and punching him play-fully in the shoulder she said, 'By! we'll have a meal the night, eh?' And to this he said, 'Give him here till I clean him.'

It was early evening before the meal was ready, and they had just finished big platters of the stewed hare when a knock came on the back door. They stared at each other, startled. Swiftly gathering the bones together, they threw them into the fire and Norah Gillespie raked some wood over them, then nodded to Sandy, and he went and opened the door.

Surprised, he saw standing there the biggest of the Mullen boys. They looked at each other for a full minute before the boy said in stilted tones, 'Thout to come an' warn you. Me da's comin' along the road. He's got a skinful; hasn't slept it off. The lads told him that you belted them; I would clear out for a time if I was you.'

Again they stared at each other; and now Sandy said, 'Thanks for tellin' me, but ... but I'm not going to run.'

The boy shook his head now, then muttered under his breath, 'He's dirty, me da, I mean in a fight.'

'I'll risk it.'

The boy still stood, then after a moment he said, 'Me name's Stan.'

'Mine's Sandy.'

They nodded at each other and half smiled, then the boy looked to where Mrs Gillespie was now standing behind Sandy, and he gulped in his throat as she said gently, 'Thank you, lad.' And she added, 'Don't be afraid for us.'

'He's mean.' The boy had his head down now and Norah Gillespie looked pityingly on him for having to admit this about his own father. She said, 'Don't worry; we can take care of ourselves.' And on this he nodded and was about to turn away when she ended, 'You'll be welcome in here any time, boy.'

The sad grey eyes were turned on her and then on Sandy, and when Sandy nodded, confirming his mother's invitation, Stan drooped his head still further, then hurried out of the yard.

They had hardly entered the room and had no time to discuss any plan they might use when there was a bawling in the street outside and Big Mullen was hammering on the door again.

When Norah Gillespie, after straightening her shoulders, made to open the door, Sandy pulled on her arm, saying, 'Let me deal with him.'

'Don't be silly, he's dangerous.'

'Look!' Sandy was hissing into her face. 'You've told me often enough in the last few days I'm a man. Well, now let me act as one.'

They stared at each other in the dim light and Norah Gillespie's face worked with the pain of indecision; but it was as he said, he was coming on sixteen years old, and a man. She stood aside.

Sandy pulled open the door as Big Mullen had his fist raised to bang on it again, and he held it in mid air as Sandy demanded in a voice from which he could scarcely keep the tremor, 'What you after?'

'Aw! It's master big-boy himsel', is it? I'll tell you what I'm after.' Big Mullen swayed back and forward. 'I'm after your hide an' I'm go-na get it, I'm go-na skin you.'

'We'll see about that.'

It's possible to say that Big Mullen got the first real surprise of his life when Sandy's hand came out and thrust him backwards. Through blinking gin-bemused gaze he watched the young fellow move into the middle of the road, and when he said 'Well, I'm ready for your skinnin',' his mouth dropped into a gape. But he didn't laugh this time, he was being shown up by a skite of a youngster, and in front of his own lads at that. But the boy's steady gaze and his stance, like that of a wrestler, stayed him and he blustered now, 'I'll teach ya to pick on somebody your own size, two bits of bairns out . . . out for a Sunday ramble . . .'

'Sunday ramble!' Sandy sneered now, and repeated again, 'Sunday ramble! Bashing an old man with stones after pinching his crutch.'

The effect of Sandy's words was surprising, for Big Mullen screwed up his eyes, straightened his body, lowered his fists, and now his bellow was ear-splitting as he turned on his sons. 'What've I told ya, eh? What've I told ya? Leave him alone. I told you to lay off Mad Mark, didn't I? . . . GET!' He made a dive at the boys and they were off like lightning, scrambling in different directions.

Big Mullen now looked at Sandy; then, his head rolling on his shoulders, he spat into the road, turned on his heel and went his wavering way down to the end house. And Sandy, perplexed, full of relief and feeling not a little sick, followed his mother into the cottage: and there they looked at each other and Norah Gillespie said, 'Well, what do you make of that? And Sandy answered, 'You're asking me.'

'By!' She drew her body up to its proud height, and her eyes passed over him lovingly as she said, 'He'll know who he's got to deal with in future, eh?' And he answered her, 'Aye, he will that.' But to himself he only hoped so, for Big Mullen drunk and Big Mullen sober were two different people, and although equally vicious he didn't know whom he feared the more.

His mother was saying now, 'Big Mullen or no Big

Mullen, we must get ready for the mornin'; it'll be an early start. I only hope we don't sleep in because we must be at the cross-roads by four o'clock.'

Be at the cross-roads at four o'clock. Sandy sighed. Every day, the summer-long now, they'd have to be at the cross roads at four o'clock to meet up with the gangs of farm workers the gaffers gathered from the different villages and let out to the farmers. He hoped tomorrow's tramp wouldn't be a long one. He had heard tell it could be as much as eight miles each way. . . .

The long twilight was flowing into darkness when Norah Gillespie called from the room to Sandy who was standing at the doorway, saying, 'Isn't it time you were turning in? I told you, you need all the sleep you can get.'

'It's too warm,' he said; 'you can hardly breathe.'

He could just make out the hummocks on the fells and in his mind's eye he saw The Nipper galloping free there. Where would he be now? Sold to some farmer who would work him to death? Dead, his throat slit, or his head battered with a hammer until he was senseless. He closed his eyes tight, shutting out the thought and the fells; then he opened them quickly again and glanced down the road, someone had come out of the Mullen's doorway and was running up the street. It was the boy, Stan, and now his father was after him.

Sandy withdrew quickly into the shadow of the doorway as he heard the voice of Big Mullen say, 'Hold your hand. Wait a minute. Look; come here.' They were only two doors down and he surmised rather than saw Stan being pulled into the wrecked cottage. He was on the point of moving out into the road when he heard footsteps on it, and with a lightning movement he stepped back into the room and closed the door, signalling to his mother by his hand on her arm to be quiet, for she had come to his side to find out what was the matter.

He heard the quiet step pause outside the door, then after a few minutes it retreated again; and now he whispered in his mother's ear, 'Stay where you are,' and tugging himself away from her now restraining hands, he opened the door and looked cautiously into the street.

The darkness was almost total now and, edging along the wall to the next cottage and standing within the shelter of the doorless aperture, he listened to the hushed voices coming through the broken wall. Stan was saying, 'It's too dark, I'll never find him,' and his father replied, 'Take the lantern.'

'I wouldn't know where to look,' Stan's voice said again. 'He could be in any of six places.'

'Look, lad.' The tone of Big Mullen's voice surprised Sandy for although it was urgent it was quiet, placating. 'You've got to find him and put things right with him; tell him the young 'uns meant no harm. Tell him I've skinned 'em an' they'll not trouble him again. Then ... then tap him as to where it is, coaxing like.'

'He'll not tell me, I've told you afore.'

'Look, lad.' Big Mullen's tone was changing now. 'I've warned you what'll happen, either you get it out of him quiet, or it'll be knocked out of him. We mean business; time's past for talkin'. It'll save a lot of trouble if he shows us the way.'

'It'll mean more trouble,' said Stan now, 'if he does show you the way; you'll land up in Australia the lot of you, or at the end of ropes.'

'We'll take our chance on that. This is the only way we can show 'em, the big boss in particular, we mean business.'

33

Sandy waited for Stan's answer to this but it didn't come, and then Big Mullen's voice was saying, 'I'll get you a light; the quicker you find him the quicker you can come back. But you've got to find him, you hear?'

He heard the steps move cautiously into the road, then fade into the distance, and after a moment he went out into the street again and, groping his way back along the wall, came to his own door. It was open and his mother was waiting and she whispered at him, 'What do you think you're up to?'

When he was inside and the door bolted he moved forward into the light of the tallow candle and shook his head as he said, 'It isn't me that's up to something, it's him, the father. He's making Stan go and find the old man, the one who gave me the hare, you know. He wants some information out of him.'

'What kind of information?'

'I don't know except it seems that the old man knows some road or passage to some place, but I couldn't gather where.'

'He's a bad 'un, that one,' said Norah Gillespie now. 'Keep clear of him. Oh!' she sighed; 'I wish we could get out of here. But there, we'll have to put up with it for the meantime. Now let's get to bed without more ado, else we'll be fit for nothing the morrow.'

Sandy did her bidding, but he couldn't sleep. First he would wonder what Big Mullen was up to; then his mind would be filled with thoughts of The Nipper. The two things seemed poles apart; he wasn't to know how soon and how vitally they were to be connected.

Three

For five days they had trudged the six miles each morning to Farmer Watson's fields and picked strawberries and dragged themselves back at night, almost too tired to get a fire going and make a meal, yet over the last three days they had been able to bank down the fire with slack coal, as Sandy was doing now, sprinkling the hot embers with wet tea leaves and the peelings from last night's potatoes, then packing the coal well down on top and hoping it would not burn through too quickly and, by the time they returned in the evening, there would be enough left to blow into flames.

He should, he knew, be grateful for the coal and the knowledge that the coal-house was half full, but he wasn't, for it had come by a means that held deep significance, frightening significance.

On Tuesday evening when they had returned from work, there, outside the front door, had lain a full load of pit coal – as the dusty slack coal was known – and as he and his mother stood looking at it Big Mullen had come out of his door, as if he had been waiting for them, and, sauntering towards them, had said, 'Evenin' missis.' And for answer his mother had asked, 'Have I you to thank for this?' She had pointed to the coal.

'Aye,' he said; 'you could say that.'

'How much?' his mother had asked.

'Aw, nowt,' he had grinned at her, showing his black tobacco-stained teeth. 'Call it a present.'

'I don't take presents, Mr Mullen, I pay for what I get. How much?'

The grin had still remained on Big Mullen's face while he looked at her admiringly, then said, 'Well, if that's how you feel, make it sixpence.'

She had turned her back on him, lifted her skirt and taken her chamois purse from her petticoat pocket. When she turned to him again she was holding out her hand and in it was a shilling and she said, 'Take that for it, it's worth more than sixpence.'

He had tossed the shilling in the palm of his hand, while keeping his eyes on her and saying, 'Always did admire independence.' Then he had added, 'Been a long day. Some trek that is to Watson's farm. 'Tisn't right; a woman like you should be at home keeping the house tidy.'

His mother was thrusting the key in the lock and he himself was staring grim-visaged at the dirty smelly man, although it was evident he had washed his face tonight, when he said, 'I earn fourteen bob a week. What do you think of that? More at times. An' the lads never less than nineteen bob atween them. That's money.' He jerked his head.

His mother had the door open now and before she stepped into the room she turned and looked at Mr Mullen and said coldly, 'You're welcome to it.'

When the door was closed Sandy stood with his back to it and watched her leaning over the table, her hands gripping the edge, and he knew a moment of deep fear, for he saw she was trembling. . . .

But now it was Saturday and tomorrow would be his. Tomorrow he'd take another long tramp, to Hursthill

Manor Farm this time, and he'd see Katie and she would tell him what had happened to The Nipper... That's if she knew.

They locked the door and went out into the dark morning. There was a warm drizzle falling and they put split sacks over their heads to keep their shoulders dry.

Ten minutes later when they came to the by-pass outside the village of Hebburn, Sandy made out, through the lifting light, the small groups huddled together round the bole of an oak tree, trying to get a little shelter from the rain. There were muttered greetings as they came up, and then they stood in silence like the rest, waiting; no one talked first thing in the morning.

Five minutes later the light had lifted enough for them to discern the ganger coming from the village, a broken line of people straggling behind him. He did not stop when he came opposite the tree and the group moved forward and joined in the cavalcade, and along the road here and there people also came from side lanes or over the open fells and joined them.

Half-an-hour later, when they reached the cross-roads, another group was waiting for them. And now the ganger, standing before them, said, 'There'll only be need of a dozen at Watson's to finish off the strawberries.' Then he pointed. 'You, Mrs Clark and your three; Peter and Matt.' He pointed to two men. 'The Scallen bairns.' His finger now moved to where a girl of about twelve was standing with three small children around her, the youngest no more than eight. Then he nodded towards two ragged youths and ended, 'And the twins. And mind—' his voice became harsh – 'don't think that because I'm not with you, you can land there late; he'll tell me your times and I'll dock it off you next week, that's if I set you on, understand?' A silence greeted this threat.

Then, his gaze moving around the rest of the company which numbered about thirty, he said, 'We're goin' to Stockwell's place. That should please some of you, only four miles off. You're going to get it easy the day.'

At the name Stockwell, Sandy and his mother glanced sharply at each other, then smiled. As they moved off he no longer trudged, but his step had a lightness to it. Stockwell's, Hursthill Manor Farm. He wouldn't have to wait until the morrow and take another long trek; he would likely see Katie the day. If he didn't see her through working hours then they would stay behind and say how-do-you-do to their late master and mistress and he would talk to Katie.

The four miles to the Manor seemed no distance to Sandy; and then he was standing in a queue in the yard waiting for his basket, but all the while looking round for the sight of Farmer Blyth or Katie. He didn't hope to see Mrs Blyth because she'd likely be indoors busy.

But he didn't see either Mr Blyth or Katie. What he did see though was a great deal of activity; big buckets of hot mash being carried into the stables, boys in the harness room polishing and rubbing, a gig being cleaned in the yard, a great herd of cows being brought in from the meadow, and the sound of girls' laughter coming from the dairy, and overall a cleanness that amazed him.

Farmer Blyth had been clean, always seeing to it that his animals lay dry and comfortable, but his yard had been a mud yard and everything was subject to weather, here the yard was made up of great slabs of stone sloping towards the gutter running along its middle length.

A large basket on each arm, he walked now by the side of his mother, and with the rest of the company along a tree-shaded lane with paddocks on each side in which horses grazed, not shires these, but sleek, long thin-legged animals that made him want to stand and gaze at them. They mounted a hill now and when they were at the top he saw to the right of him vegetable and fruit gardens set out in such precise order that he was again astounded by the neatness. As his eye roved round it was halted by the sight of a great stone house in the far distance. The rain had stopped and the morning sun was gleaming on it, turning the colour of the stone into a soft rose pearl which gave it an ethereal appearance as if it was afloat. That must be the Manor House, Hurst-hill Manor. A big house like that for only three people to live in. That's what they'd said on the road. There were only Sir William Stockwell and his wife and daughter; and then they didn't always live there. Six to eight months of the year they were away, but they always came in the shooting season for a couple of months, and he gathered from the chatter that there were great goings on, because Sir William Stockwell was very partial to parties. The staff had always to be prepared for him having a party within two or three days of his arrival. It was said there were forty servants all told in the Manor and stables; that wasn't counting the farm.

As he dragged his eyes away from the house and went down the hill to the gardens, he thought it must make a man feel like a God to live like that.

The agricultural labouring gangs were supposed to be supplied with food besides the shilling a day earned by adults, ninepence for those over twelve and under sixteen, and sixpence for those up to twelve years old. The food consisted of a dollop of thick porridge at eight o'clock, a plate of bean and vegetable soup, often cooked in the boiler where the pigs' swill was prepared, at twelve, and at half past four in the afternoon two slices of rye bread and pig fat for adults, and one for children.

The field fare, as it was called, was no better at the Manor farm than at any other place, with one exception, they could have milk with their porridge and with their half past four bread, tea if they so desired ... and they all so desired.

It was when two maids brought the bread, milk and tea to the field that Sandy saw from the distance that one of them limped. With a feeling of joy he dropped his basket and ran towards Katie, and her surprise and pleasure were as great as his. 'Why! Sandy; I never knew, I would have come at dinner-time. Oh, how are you?'

'Fine, Katie.' He stood before her rubbing the palms of his fruit-dyed hands together. 'An' you?'

'I'm fine too, Sandy. Yes, yes, I'm fine.'

'You're settling?'

'Yes; and Father is an' all. It's much better than he thought, but—' she shook her head – 'Mother isn't taking it too well. She can't get over not being mistress in her own house. But Mrs Armstrong, the farmer's wife, she's quite good, fair to work for. And—' she leant towards him whispering now, 'we may get a cottage, a really decent one. One of the men has moved; he was assistant to Mr Armstrong.' She looked at him regretfully now. 'If only Father had been here a little longer he might have been offered the post, but there.' She shrugged her thin shoulders. 'You never know. We'll have patience. How's your mother? Where is she, is she here?' She looked about her.

'Yes.' He pointed towards a long row of raspberry canes. 'Here she comes.' Then turning to her again, he said quickly, 'Did ... did you find out anything, Katie, about ... about The Nipper, I mean?' He watched her lips droop and her eyes lower, and he whispered, 'He's not . . . they didn't?'

'No. No.' She was looking at him again. 'They didn't kill him, but . . . but . . .' She paused for a long moment and then said, 'He was sold for a pit pony.'

'A PIT PONY!' He narrowed his eyes and drew in his chin, 'The Nipper, a pit pony? He'd never be able to stand it. Oh lord!' Now his head was bowed and was swinging from side to side only to stop abruptly as he asked, 'Which pit, do you know?'

'The Beulah, yon side of Hebburn I think. It belongs to our master, Sir William Stockwell I mean.'

'The Beulah.' He was repeating the name softly. The Beulah was but two miles from them. It was where the Mullens worked. He had a picture of the two young ones goading The Nipper, and again his head was hanging.

It was his mother's voice that brought it up this time. She was calling over the distance, 'Oh, hello, Miss Katie. Oh, it is nice to see you. I was going to call later, after we've done, and see the mistress an' the master. How are they?'

'Very well, Norah. Oh, and it's nice to see you again.' Katie's hands went out impulsively, and Norah Gillespie held them tightly in her own as she gazed down on the sweet face of the girl she almost thought of as her own, for she had brought her up side by side with Sandy.

The other maid was moving away now and calling to Katie, and she looked back and said, 'I'm coming, I'm coming.' Then glancing from Sandy to his mother, she said, 'I'll tell mother and father. You'll come and see them before you go, won't you?' And Norah Gillespie said, 'Of course, of course.' But all Sandy did was to nod at Katie, and she stared at him in understanding for a moment before turning and limping away.

'Isn't it lovely to see her again?' Norah sat down on the side of a bank and munched slowly at her bread and fat, and when Sandy didn't answer her she looked towards him, where he was sitting with his knees up, his elbows resting on them, and the bread hanging loosely in his hands, and she asked 'What's the matter with you?'

Slowly he turned his head towards her. 'The Nipper's been sold for a pit pony.'

Her mouth worked, her chin wobbled but she said nothing. She just looked ahead now, and his voice came to her, his tone full of anguish. 'He's down the Beulah mine, the Beulah where the Mullens work.

He watched her head wag as if with impatience and when she turned to him and said harshly under her breath, 'Well, at least you know he's not dead,' he answered bitterly, 'He might as well be, down there for ever, until they bring him up stiff.'

'I've told you, boy, there's nothing you can do about him, so for your sake and mine you've got to forget him, because I can't live along of you moping all the time, I've enough to worry me wonderin' how we're going to exist without you gnawing your innards out for a dratted undersized horse that didn't belong to you in the first place.'

His body jerked towards her, his mouth was full of words, but she held his eyes and he knew what she said was true, every word; except one thing, there was something he could do about it.

As the idea grew larger in his mind, he looked up at the great stretch of sky that seemed to go on for ever and ever, and it was as if he were seeing it for the first and last time.

Four

It was late on the Saturday night when he told her what he intended to do. They were both in bed and he sat up in the darkness and said softly, 'Ma!' and she, pulling herself out of waves of sleep, said quickly, 'Yes? Yes, what is it?'

A silence fell on the room again, as heavy as the blackness, before he said, 'I'm not goin' pickin' anymore, I'm ... I'm goin' to get a new job.'

'A new job? What you talkin' about?'

'I'm ... I'm goin' down the pit.'

He heard her spring out of the bed; he heard her coming towards him, and when she fell on her knees at the side of his bed, then groped for his shoulders and gripped them, he knew fear of her for a moment.

'WHAT-DID-YOU-SAY?'

'You heard right enough, Ma, you heard.'

'Yes, I heard; and I don't want to hear it again. You go down the mine? Never! Among scum like the Mullens!'

'They're not all like the Mullens. Remember, the Robsons and the Clarks? They ... they were Jarrow miners. Dad knew them; they were all right.'

'They were exceptions. For the main part, they're like wild animals. And the things that happen down there ...

43

Anyway I'm not goin' into it, an' you're not goin' down the pit.'

'I am, Ma.'

He felt her grip slowly relaxing from his shoulders. And then she took her hands away, and now, her voice pleading, she said, 'Oh, boy! boy! Anything but that. Twelve hours a day in darkness; you don't know what you're talking about.'

'If the young Mullens can stand it, surely I can.'

'You're not the young Mullens. You are a different sort from the Mullens an' their like, I've tried to make you remember that.

'As for that dratted horse!' She was now stamping about the floor. 'You'd ruin your life for that no-good Galloway.'

'He wasn't just a horse to me, Ma.' His voice was soothingly soft. 'He could read my mind better than I could meself; an' ... an' I knew what he thought. He ... he wasn't JUST a horse.'

He heard her flop on to the bed and when her fists beat on the straw pillow he pulled the coverlet over his head and wished, oh how he wished that he didn't need to do what he had to do. But The Nipper was down the pit and that was where he was going.

His mother started again on the Sunday morning. She told him all the stories she had heard about the goings on down the pit, the ill treatment of the workhouse boys who were called apprentices. To this he answered he was no workhouse boy. When she said that the boys were sometimes kept down for twenty hours at a stretch he answered that no one would keep him down for twenty hours. When she flung at him that half his pay would have to be spent at the tommy shop – the grocery store run by the owners of the mine where everything was much dearer than in the ordinary shops – he retorted that even so, what he would have left would be more than he was earning now, and if young Bill Mullen could earn four shillings, and Joe six, and Stan nine, well he was older than Stan, and if they went by age he would likely pick up ten. Just think of that.

'I am thinking of that,' his mother replied as she looked at him sorrowfully. 'I'm also thinking that it's a pity they didn't shoot that Galloway.' And at this he turned his head away from her and they didn't speak for almost two hours.

It was on twelve o'clock – when they heard the Mullen boys out in the street – that Norah Gillespie broke the silence, saying, 'You do know that if you ask a favour of him an' he gets you set on he'll never be off this doorstep. You know that, don't you? And what will you do about it then?'

At this he had looked at her steadily and said, 'I think you'll be a better match for him than me.'

When she had closed her eyes and pressed her lips together he had gone out, her voice coming after him, crying, 'Don't sign any bond, Sandy. Please don't sign any bond.'

He walked steadily down the row and knocked on the door of the end house and when it was opened by Stan, Sandy said to him, 'Can I see your da?'

Stan's expression became apprehensive and Sandy, his voice low, muttered, 'It's all right. I ... I just want to see him about gettin' set on at the pit.'

'Set on at the pit?' Stan screwed his face up in disbelief. 'You're kiddin', aren't you?'

'No.'

Stan pulled the door closed behind him and stepped into

the street and said, 'Look, you mightn't get much in the fields, but . . . but it's a better life, clean and healthy. Have you ever been down the pit?'

Sandy shook his head.

'Well, what I say to you now is, don't.'

At this point the door was pulled open behind him and Big Mullen stood there. 'What is it?' he said, as he looked at Sandy.

Sandy's glance now wavered between Stan and his father; then taking in a deep breath he said, 'I wonder if you could get me set on at your place, Mr Mullen?'

The bleary eyes widened, the lips pushed out as if about to whistle, the head nodded, the man's whole attitude became one of condescension, and he said, 'Dare say, me word's good there. But mind.' He looked him up and down now. 'It's hard graft, not like bairns' play in the fields.'

Bairns' play in the fields. Twelve hours of back-breaking labour, sometimes wet with sweat, or wet with rain, your belly empty, your legs weak and the long trek at the end of the day. Bairns' play! He wanted to come back at this little man, but he held his peace.

Big Mullen, walking round him now as if he was an animal in a cattle market, said, 'You're too big for a putter.' He looked disparagingly at Sandy's broad back and, coming round and facing him again, he said, 'And you're too old for a trapper.' Then he added, 'It's either the coal face or up top. Course you won't get much of a screw up top; the coal face is the place.' He wagged his head now. 'That's if you're up to it.'

Sandy stared at the leering face before him, then said flatly, 'Wherever I go I'm not signing any bond.' And at this Big Mullen's eyebrows moved upwards and he said off-handedly, 'Oh well, that'll be up to you. No bond, no secure job; you could be stood off any time Later on you'd have to sign.'

'When will I know?' asked Sandy abruptly.

Big Mullen stared at him hard, then said flatly, 'Come along of us the mornin'; I'll show you to the butty.'

'The butty?'

'Aye, he's the man who'll set you on.'

'They don't have a manager?'

At this Big Mullen laughed and said, 'Oh, they've got a manager, an' an under-one, but he lets the work out to the butties and it's the butties who sets on the lads and sees that they work.' He poked his head towards Sandy now. 'You've got to have guts to work down the pit. You think you've got the guts?'

Sandy's teeth moved hard against each other before he replied, 'I've always worked hard.'

'There's hard work an' hard work, so we'll have to see, won't we?' Big Mullen now turned his back on him and made to go into the house, but paused at the door, saying, 'Tell your ma I'll get you in.' Then, his head over his shoulder, he ended, 'The shift starts at five, five till five. That's from the bottom, and we've got to get there and down. We leave here just past four. I'll give you a rap.'

When he had gone into the house the two boys looked at each other; and now Stan, his hands stuck into the pockets of his ragged, knee-length cord trousers, shook his head in bewilderment before he, too, turned away, leaving Sandy to walk dolefully back down the row.

When he got inside the house his mother's eyes were waiting for him but he said nothing, and his silence told her what she dreaded, and she bowed her head against it, and fate.

Five

Sandy had seen the outer workings of a pit before; he had watched the high wagons laden with coal rollicking down inclines with a push from a man's hands, and others being slowly dragged up inclines by the use of pulleys. He had watched the wheel that let the cage down into the earth spinning high above the top of the gantry, and he had seen men emerging from a hole in the ground all looking like black devils. He had seen all this one day when he was twelve as he stood by his father's side at the top of a slag heap, and his father had pointed and said, 'To an open-air man that is a foretaste of hell.'

And now as Sandy threaded his way behind Big Mullen his father's description was to the forefront of his mind; men and boys were milling about in the dark, their candle-lanterns swinging, elongating and distorting the shadows all over the marshalling yard. There was no sound of talking or morning greetings, only the harsh grating of the heavy boots as they struck against the iron track that ran down the middle of the yard and now and again sent sparks flying as if from a tinder.

Suddenly he lost sight of Big Mullen, and Stan pulled him sideways out of the stream and into a building where a man was sitting behind a narrow desk. Big Mullen was saying to him 'I've got a new one here, name of Gillespie. Sixteen an' a bit. He'll come to on Bonding Day all right.'

He wasn't sixteen and a bit, he wasn't sixteen for another month. And what did he mean, he'll come to on Bonding Day?

'I'm taking him down to Macintyre.'

'Sure he's not from The House; they tell me there's five missin' from Doncaster way?'

'No, he's not from The House no-where. He lives next door a me, mother's a friend o' mine.'

Sandy's teeth were gritting hard, but, his eyes catching Stan's, he saw the boy make a slight movement with his head as if to say, you can't do anything about it, so keep quiet. And this he did; in fact he was shocked into quietness a few minutes later when he was pushed into a cage with the entire Mullen family, the two younger ones unusually quiet now and still sleepy-eyed, as they dropped into the bowels of the earth.

Only Big Mullen took a delight in the rude cage's effect on Sandy and remarked as they stepped out of it, 'You'll hev to get used to it; you've seen nothin' yet.'

Sandy had expected that at the bottom of the shaft he would see a great open space with passages, which the men called roads, going off, but what he saw was an area about twelve feet wide and about twice as long, for beyond the light from the lanterns there appeared to be a black blank wall; but as far as he could see the place was filled with iron bogies on which were loaded big skips of coal. There was no sign of a Galloway as yet.

'Hi-up!' Big Mullen was pushing him between the shoulders, and he turned round quickly and only just in time stopped himself from crying, 'Don't do that!'

His eyes almost popping out of his head now, he stumbled up the uneven narrow road, then of a sudden he was brought to a gaping halt. A boy of about nine, his body bent low, his hands gripping a bogie and endeavouring to push it along the slow incline of the main road

49

was being kicked in the buttock by a man who was yelling at him, 'You should've heard the first time. B district, from the mother gate, that's where you should be. Want it easy, do you?' He lifted his booted foot again and the blow knocked the boy on to his bare knees on the rough ground, and Sandy's face twisted against the impact and the pain it must have caused.

Joe Mullen, looking up at him now and seeming to come wide awake for the first time, grinned at him as he said, 'He's always gettin' it. He's only an apprentice, daren't open his gob case he gets a boot in it an' all.'

'Shut your gob or else!' Stan was thrusting Joe forward now, and he beckoned Sandy on and again they were following Big Mullen, and all in single file.

Ten minutes later they came to a form of cross-roads and here were gathered about thirty boys ranging in ages from seven to sixteen. A man was standing with a piece of slate in his hand, scratching on it with a slate pencil, and to him Big Mullen said, 'Brought you a new 'un, Dick.'

'Oh, aye.' The man didn't look up.

'Bit big, but strong like. Do on the face I should say.'

The man now raised his eyes from the slate and looked Sandy up and down; then he said, 'Fourteen a fortnight, overtime if you want it.'

Sandy remained mute and Big Mullen said, 'Which section?' and the butty said, 'Put him on the low rake with Tom Fitzsimmons. Get him used to bending his back.'

'Aye. Aye,' said Big Mullen, grinning now.

They were walking again, Sandy stumbling and tripping as he went; yet he could not resist whispering to Stan, 'Where are the ponies?'

'The what?'

'The Galloways.'

'Oh, they'll be on the other road.'

'Don't they work along here?'

'No. This is a low haulage road.' They stepped aside at this point as confirmation of Stan's words passed them. A small boy, with a chain through his legs, one end of which was attached to the front of his belt while the other was hooked on to a bogie that was piled high with coal, was straining with all his might to keep it moving, whilst another and smaller boy, his body almost horizontal, was pushing from the back with all his small might too.

Stan's voice brought Sandy from his gaping again when he added, 'There's another two roads going off up front.' He nodded ahead. 'One goin' into A section, the other to C. Keep your eyes open so's you'll know your way about.'

Keep your eyes open, he said, when all you could see was a few feet ahead. But, his mind still on The Nipper, he asked, 'Are they well looked after?'

'Who? Oh ... ponies.' Stan screwed his face up, then shrugged one shoulder. 'Knocked about a bit. But some can hold their own. Vicious some.' Then stopping suddenly before a small door, Stan said, 'I go off here,' and Sandy had an overpowering impulse to grip his arm and say, 'No, man; don't leave me alone, not until I get used to it.' But what he said was, 'Won't ... won't I see you again till the night?'

'I'll come along at snap time.'

Sandy nodded once in thanks, then trudged on after Big Mullen, who remained silent. There were men in front and men behind and all were silent. One after the other they bent down now and went through a low four foot high door, then through a piece of flapping canvas, then through another door, and here Sandy was startled to see the eyes of a small boy, even smaller than Joe Mullen, who was sitting on the ground with a rope in his hand which was attached to the door. One of the men, nodding down at the small face, said 'Double shift, lad?' and the black head moved slowly as the lids strained to keep open.

Double shift! Sandy felt the sweat running down from his oxters. Couldn't be, not twenty-four hours for a little fellow like that. A spasm of fear shot through him as he thought he'd never be able to stand twenty-four hours down here at a time. . . .Yet that young 'un back there?

They were walking bent double now, the light from the candle-lantern showing great boulders above their heads, not of coal but of rock, and these were supported seemingly precariously by a single row of pit props at either side of the narrow tunnel.

On and on they went until Sandy thought they'd never come to the end of this back-breaking road; then the roof gradually heightened and they were standing upright once more and opposite to them was a wall of rock and to one side a passage way not more than two foot high and two and a half foot wide, and to the other, another road.

Four men were now divesting themselves of their clothes and hanging them here and there on the props, and Big Mullen, looking round, said, 'Where's Fitzsimmons?' and a tall man, coming out of the dark wall of shadow, said, 'Who wants me?'

Sandy noted that Big Mullen had a leer on his face; he also noted that the look he gave the big man wasn't friendly; but there was a note of laughter in his voice as he said, 'Brought you a new marrer.' He laid stress on the word marrer. 'Macintyre says to start him here.'

The big man gave Sandy a sidelong glance then said, 'Good enough.' And on this Big Mullen turned away and went down the side road without any further word to Sandy, and the big man said, 'Get your clothes off, lad, unless you want them to stick to you.'

'All of them?'

'Aye, all of them. Keep your linings on if you're modest. Have you got any linings?'

'Aye; short 'uns.'

There was laughter among the men now, but it was checked by the big man saying, 'Well, let's get goin'. And you, lad—' he pointed towards Sandy where he was scrambling out of his clothes – 'follow us in.'

Follow them in, he had said. Through this little hole? But they had got through; they had seemed to fold up, melt into it.

His shoulders were no sooner in the passage way than he wanted to cry out as the rough stones scraped his bare flesh. Then a voice from above him said, 'Fold in your chest, lad,' and two hands came on his and pushed his shoulders downwards; only then did he realize that he had come through into an open space. But . . . but what an open space! It wasn't high enough to stand up in. The lanterns showed the broken coal face for a distance of about five yards, beyond was nothing, at least not that he could see.

'You're my marrer,' said the big man now with a laugh, 'so you'll have to learn to act like me marrer an' look slippy. By the way, me name's Tom Fitzsimmons.' Now his hand came out and smacked Sandy on the chest sharply as he said, 'Don't look so scared, lad, there's nobody goin' to murder you. The only thing I want out of you is your sweat, an' I'll get that, if nowt else.' He was kneeling now on the rough surface of the floor and he struck at the coal face, bringing down a great sharp wedge of coal, then turning to Sandy, he said, 'You see the idea? As I get it out you move it, then pass it along to Jimmy.' He nodded towards a small, bright-faced naked man. 'And he passes it out to the skips. Get it?'

'Yes, Sir.'

At this not only did the big man laugh but so did all the men on the coal face, and Tom Fitzsimmons, slapping him on the back now, said, 'Well, lad, that's the first time I've been given a title; I only hope it's a sign of things to come.' Then his voice dropping, he said, 'Tom will be good enough to be gettin' on with, eh lad?'

Sandy nodded, glad that the sweat that was already pouring from him in the humid atmosphere was hiding his blushing face. But one thing he knew already and was thankful for, he liked this man, this Tom Fitzsimmons. . . .

But three hours later at eight o'clock there was only one thought in his mind which was that he would die if this went on any longer. Every bone in his body was aching, and his eyes were smarting unbearably with a mixture of coal dust and salt sweat, and he knew his mother, and even Big Mullen, had been right, life in the fields was child's play to this. The man to whom he had taken a liking now appeared ruthless and untiring, for his arms were like a machine, lifting the pick, banging it into the coal face, pressing down, pulling, lifting again, on and on ceaselessly.

'There, that'll do for a start. Now for a snap. . . . Feeling it, lad?'

Sandy wiped the sweat from his eyes with the back of his hand, blinked painfully and muttered, 'I'm new to it, it'll come.'

'Aye, it'll come. This day week an' you'll be in your stride. You got any bait?'

'Yes.'

'Well, go along out and eat it.'

In the roadway the men were sitting together on their hunkers munching and talking. Sandy sat by himself waiting for Stan, but he had almost finished his bread and dripping before Stan put in an appearance. He came out of the black shadows and looked about him, and seeing Sandy, he was making his way towards him when Tom Fitzsimmons's voice came at him, saying, 'Lost your way?'

'No.' Stan's voice was quiet, tentative, 'Just wanted a word with Sandy, pal of mine.'

Tom Fitzsimmons looked at him hard before turning his gaze away; and Stan, sitting down beside Sandy, bowed his head and muttered under his breath, 'He's no truck with us.'

'Why?' asked Sandy in a whisper.

'Aw, you know.' Stan shrugged his shoulders. 'Me da. An' me da's for a strike, always is, but Tom Fitzsimmons has other ideas. He just wants to talk; thinks you can get things done that way.' He shook his head. 'I don't know.'

'Stan.'

'Aye?'

'Are the ponies out yet?'

'Ponies?' Stan's face crinkled. 'Why are you always on about ponies?'

'Aw.' Sandy shook his head. 'I was used to them on the farm. I like ponies, I just thought I'd like to have a look at them.'

'Well, you won't see them down this road ever. The level's too low; the bairns push the bogies up to the drift, then they hook the ponies on for the long pull. They still need the bairns behind them though, for those bogies carry some.'

'Could I see them there, at – at the drift?'

'Aye, you could. Come along at middle snap, you get

half-an-hour then. They get their bait an' all around that time.'

'Ta, I will.'

'How . . . how you gettin' on?'

'Oh.' Sandy let out a long breath. 'I'll get used to it I suppose. Bit tirin'.'

'You're lucky.'

'What do you mean, lucky?'

'To start along o' Tom Fitzsimmons. He goes easy on you, the young 'uns.'

Easy! If the last three hours had been easy, he wouldn't want to be with anyone who worked him hard.

'I wish I was in your shoes.'

As Sandy was staring at his new, solemn-faced, enigmatic friend, Tom Fitzsimmons cried, 'Well, get off your velvet couches, lads, and let's take a gentle stroll inbye.'

'Ta-rah,' said Stan, hastily, at this, and Sandy answered, 'Ta-rah,' and in a few minutes he was back on the face, forcing his body to go through the same motions over and over; bend, lift, thrust; bend, lift, thrust. Sometimes the rhythm would go smoothly until he would slip on to the knife-edged fragments under his feet and fall awkwardly under the weight of the coal.

By twelve o'clock he was bleeding in several places and he was thinking for the hundredth time, I can't stand it, I can't stand it, when Tom Fitzsimmons said, 'Well, lads, enough's enough,' and they were crawling through the low aperture again and into the road.

He had difficulty in asking a first request of Tom Fitzsimmons, for his throat was clogged with dust and his body was weakened with work and sweat. 'Can . . . can I,' he began, 'can I go along to the drift, to see . . . to see Stan?'

Tom Fitzsimmons was gazing down at him intently

now, his eyes looking white in his dead black face, and he said, 'Aye, lad. The next thirty minutes you can do as you like. But do you mind if I give you a word of warnin'?'

Sandy waited.

'The Mullens will do you no good.'

'I know that. But Stan, he's . . . he's different, he doesn't hold with his da. I'm sure of that.'

'You think not?' It was a question to which no answer seemed necessary, for Tom Fitzsimmons's tone conveyed that he thought that if Stan was Big Mullen's son then he was tarred with the same brush.

'I think he's all right.'

'Well, every man to his own opinion. I just thought I'd give you a word.'

'Thanks, an' I'll remember.'

'Do that, lad. And remember another thing.' He checked Sandy as he was turning away. 'If you're five minutes late, 'I'll skin your hide.' The threat was issued with a smile, and Sandy managed to smile back before he turned and staggered up the roadway to the drift, with Tom's voice coming after him, saying lightly, 'An' don't keep rubbin' the bloody patches, you're only rubbing the muck in. Let them bleed, they'll clean themselves.'

There was a new boy sitting in the darkness at the air gate. In the light of the lantern he looked all eyes and mouth. He never spoke as he pulled on the rope, and as Sandy went through the door he half turned and looked at him again and the feeling that came into his chest disturbed him. He didn't put the name compassion to it, he only knew that the little fellow sitting there made him feel even more sad than had the first one he had seen.

At the drift top which was the junction of a number of roads, Sandy saw Stan sitting alongside three boys.

There were another five men sitting on their hunkers with their backs against the opposite wall, and standing, one facing up the main road and one facing down, were two Galloways, both harnessed to bogies, and Sandy felt his heart leap as if it was going to burst through his rib cage when he recognized that the one facing uphill was The Nipper.

'How's it going?' Stan's voice drew his eyes away from the hanging, dejected head and, walking slowly towards him but not looking at him, he answered, 'Not too bad.'

As Stan said, 'These are me mates, Fred, Dixie and Paul,' Sandy turned away without acknowledging the boys and began walking towards the small horse.

'Keep away from him.' The voice came from one of the men, and Sandy stopped and looked towards him and the man said, 'He'll kick you in the teeth as soon as look at you, he's fresh.'

'He won't kick me.' He was sorry as soon as he uttered the words, for the man pulled himself to his feet and said slowly, 'He won't kick you, huh! Who do you think you are, God Almighty? Look.' He pointed. 'He's got his head up, an' when he's got his head up he means business.'

And The Nipper had his head up, for he had recognized the voice, the voice of his friend.

The group of men and boys were all now startled by a loud prolonged neigh.

'See what I mean?' said the miner, turning to Big Mullen, and Big Mullen, coming and standing beside him, said, 'Aye, John. Aye, I hear he's a bad 'un.'

Sandy looked at Big Mullen, then at the man called John and the other two men who had joined them, then his eyes swung to the boys who were now coming from their corner. He knew he'd have to speak to The Nipper, make himself known to him, but he'd have to give some sort of explanation to this crowd afore he could do it, so he said, 'I've . . . I've got a way with animals.'

There was a derisive laugh now from an ugly, stumpy looking man, who turned to Big Mullen and said, 'This youngster you brought in, he's got a way with animals, Mac?' and Big Mullen laughed and said, 'Aye. Well, he'd better show us then, Peter, hadn't he?' And the man replied, 'Aye, he'd better;' then he said to Sandy, 'Go on, show us the way you've got with animals, lad. I'll bet you. . . .' He looked round for something to bet on. 'I'll bet you me bait.' He pointed to a wooden box. 'There's bacon in there, an' legs of rabbit. Go on, if he doesn't kick you in the teeth that bait's yours.'

Sandy waited a moment, pretending to hesitate. He looked around at the faces. They were all grinning, all except Stan's, and Stan made an almost imperceptible movement with his head, telling him not to try it, because The Nipper was now tossing his mane and trying to free himself from where his reins were attached to a post.

Slowly Sandy moved forward and, stopping within a foot of the horse, said softly, 'Hello there, lad,' and his hand went out and stroked the sweaty muzzle. Then he moved another step and drew his hand down the animal's neck, and felt the quivering of its whole body going through his own. Then he slid his arm right round its neck, talking all the time. 'There now. There now. You're goin' to be all right. Just stay put, stay quiet.' When at last he moved away from the horse it was quiet, and so were the spectators.

'Well I'll be damned!' It was a thin man speaking now. He was noticeable for his big head and long arms, and something else, his Irish voice, and he looked around the men and said, 'That boy's got a charm on him, that's what he has, a charm on him. He could never have done it else. He's got a charm on him. What you carryin'?' he now asked Sandy. And Sandy said, 'Carrying? What do you mean?'

'Have you a relic on you, the finger nail of a saint or somethin' like?'

'No.' Sandy's nose wrinkled. 'Why would I want that?'

'Just 'cos you did a miracle with that animal there, and you could never do it off your own bat, I'll swear on it, because I've seen him not an hour gone tryin' to kick the daylights out of Nick Stock, an' what Nick Stock doesn't know about horses isn't worth learnin', for it's his work. If it had been me he had went for I'd have had his innards out with me pick, I would that.'

Peter Armstrong was holding out his bait box to Sandy now, and Sandy, pushing it away, said, 'No, I don't want that.'

'Go on, you won it fair.'

Again the box was thrust under his nose, and he looked down on slices of bread, a thick collop of bacon and two rabbit's legs and his mouth watered; but again he pushed it away from him, saying, 'I've me own bait, thanks.'

'Aw well.' The man seemed relieved. 'I tried to pay me bet, you can't say I didn't.'

'That's all right,' said Sandy, and he was turning with the other boys to go to the corner and sit down when The Nipper again neighed and Stan said, 'It was as if he knew you, as if he was talking to you.'

'Aye,' said Sandy, 'it was, wasn't it?' and the thought came to him that he could confide in Stan and he would do, but later on.

Having sat down and started on his bait, he asked

casually, 'Who's in charge of that one?' He nodded towards The Nipper.

'Paul here,' said Stan. 'Paul Bowmer.'

Sandy looked at Paul. He was a boy of eleven or twelve. He had a dull face, but he didn't look vicious. Paul said, 'I've had a devil of a job with him this last week; I've tried everythin'.' He leant forward and whispered, 'How d'you do it?'

Sandy looked back into the small round eyes and said slowly, 'Kindness. Think kindly towards them and they pick it up, you know, sort of sense it.'

'No kiddin'?'

'No kiddin'.'

'I've just got to think about bein' kind to him and he'll act for me like he did you?'

Sandy paused, looked about him, then let his eyes rest on The Nipper, and he said, 'Well, it'll take a little time, but he'll get used to you. I'll—' he laughed now as if he was making a joke – 'I'll have a word with him afore you start.'

'Ta.' The boy took him quite seriously and again said, 'Ta.' Then he added, 'Did you see wor Teddy inbye, on the door?'

'You mean in there?' Sandy pointed, and Paul nodded. 'Yes, I saw him.'

Paul now edged himself towards him. 'Will you, when you're passin', stop and have a word with him, I mean stay a second or so if you can? You see he's new to it and scared an' they don't like me goin' near him, stops them bein' broken in they say; but it gets lonely sittin' by yersel', and he's too young to start puttin' yet, so if you'll give him a word?'

'Aye, I will.'

The boy, Paul, nodded and sat back and started tear-

61

ing at a piece of dark-looking bread. And now he said, as if to himself and not by way of explanation, 'He was just apprenticed last week.'

Apprenticed. That meant he was from the workhouse. The pain in Sandy's chest deepened and it came to him that he had entered a new world, a new phase of his life.

Six

During his first week down the mine Sandy learned a number of things. First, that labour was comparative. The backaching weariness that was engendered by working in the fields was not to be compared with the body-racking pain and the feeling of utter exhaustion left by twelve hours down the mine.

The first night when he had come up above ground he had staggered about like a drunken man; it was as if the air had intoxicated him, and the Mullens had laughed their heads off; even Stan had been amused, and when he reached home he had thrown himself down on the floor covered from head to foot with coal dust and dried blood as he was, and gone fast asleep. And there his mother had found him when she came in from the fields an hour later, and he had woken to her whimpering, 'Oh my God! boy, look! Look at the sight of you, blood and muck.' He was too exhausted to push at her hands as she washed him down.

The second thing he learned was that men fought differently down the mine. He had witnessed two fights, one between boys and one between men. When the boys fought Big Mullen and his pals formed a ring round them and egged them on, and they fought with feet and teeth and hands like claws, seeming bent on tearing each other's eyes out.

The men fought with their bare fists, and with their knees they struck out at all the lower parts of the body. It was after witnessing a fight that he learned there were two warring factions down the mine, one headed by Big Mullen, the other by Tom Fitzsimmons. He also learned that there was a strike imminent.

He had sat and listened to Tom Fitzsimmons, Jimmy Tyler, Chris Suggett and Fred Jamieson as they talked openly about their grievances, the main grievance being that the corves of coal they sent from the face were too often short weighed by the keeker – this was the name given to the check weighman who, if he found a little slate or stone amongst the coal in the seven and a half hundredweight basket, would discard the whole corve, so giving free coal to the owners and a bonus to himself. Added to this, men working on bank – above ground – wanted a standard wage of three ha'pence an hour. There was also a crying need for better safety conditions underground, and every man wanted the wording of the bond altered, the bond that tied a man to the mine for a year and assured him of work at a promised rate, but at the same time had loopholes which allowed the owners to cut wages when they deemed it necessary, which often happened when another pit closed and its miners were looking for work.

They wanted the pernicious rule – that a man could be fined or even jailed for staying off work – done away with: it was little use a man saying he was sick, he had to prove it, and how could he do that when he hadn't the money to send for a doctor, and there was only his word for it? They wanted the maximum time a child should work down the mine to be twelve hours, no overtime until he was fourteen.

All this talk seemed reasonable to Sandy's ears, but

when he went to the middle drift and strained to hear Big Mullen, Felton, Armstrong and Casey talking he knew, without being able to distinguish all they said, that whatever they were planning wasn't reasonable and could only lead to trouble, for repeatedly he would hear phrases like, 'Talkin's no good. The time for talkin's past, it's action we want, action.' Then one day another word was added to the word action . . . the word was, loud. 'Loud action,' they said, and following this there was a silence, and then a series of mutterings of 'Aye. Aye, that would do it.' Loud action. Sandy could make no sense of this.

The next thing he learned was that some horses took to working down the mine, or became resigned to it, while others never did. One was Paddy The Kick. He was smaller than The Nipper, and full of fight, although he was eight years old. They said his back legs had broken more shins than falls of stone. Big Mullen had egged Sandy on to test his powers on Paddy The Kick, but Sandy had demurred, saying, 'One at a time; I'll take one at a time.'

Then there was Sniffy, a bony, body-scarred horse, that sniffed loudly up its nostrils before kicking out with its hooves. Cock-Eye was an old horse, blind in one eye; Sandy couldn't bear to ask how this had come about. Cock-Eye was docile, as was Mary Ann, but Bella was spirited and didn't like being handled by anybody except Fred Beecham, and he, in his way, was kind to her.

One thing that pained Sandy was the fact that all these five horses had been down in the dark for years, never glimpsing the sky or munching a bit of green grass, though he had to admit that their feed wasn't bad.

He had inveigled himself into the good books of Nick Stock who had heard about his handling of The Nipper. Nick Stock was a dour man, a Scot from across the Border; he had chest trouble, the result of years spent on the coal face, and had now the comparatively light job of horsekeeper.

On Sandy's first visit to the stables – this was after he had finished his shift at the end of his fourth day – Nick Stock had seemed slightly resentful of his power over The Nipper, but Sandy had been sensible enough to praise the horse boxes and the fact that there was dry straw in them.

On this first Saturday morning he asked his mother for threepence. Without question she gave it to him, and that night, at the end of the shift, when all the men were scrambling upwards to receive their pay, he went to the stables and there, handing tuppence to Nick Stock said, 'Get yourself a mug of beer.' Then proffering a further penny he added, 'And could I have a penn'orth of carrots from your land?'

He had learned that Nick had a patch of land on which he grew his own vegetables. This was unusual as most mine owners did not allow the miners to cultivate land; but this patch had belonged to Nick's people who had been blacksmiths.

Nick Stock held the threepence in his hand, then looked at Sandy and said, 'It's kind of you, lad, right kind.' Threepence wasn't to be sneezed at when you knew you could never earn more than nine shillings a week.

Sandy jerked his head, then asked, 'Will it run to one for each of them?'

'I should say it will, lad.'

They smiled at each other; then Sandy went to The Nipper, put his arms round his neck and spoke to him, and The Nipper nuzzled him.

Looking on in amazement, Nick Stock said, 'Try it on the others, lad; try it on Paddy.'

Sandy looked hard at the horsekeeper now, and feeling

he could trust this man, he said, 'I couldn't do it with any but this one, Mr Stock; you see he was my pony on the farm afore me master went bust. I . . . I had trained him.'

Nick Stock coughed, spat into the dust, then ran his hand through his hair, after which he smiled slowly and asked quietly, 'Is that why you came down, lad?' And Sandy nodded. Then Nick Stock put his hand on his shoulder and said, 'You're a lad after me own heart. Don't you worry, I'll see he's all right.'

'You won't let on?'

'No lad, I won't let on, not to a soul, we'll go on lettin' Mike Casey think you've got a relic on you.'

They laughed together and Sandy went out with a full throat but happier than he had been for a long while. He had made friends with the most important man in the mine, at least the most important to him. If only he could have taken The Nipper up into the light. But it was doubtful if The Nipper would ever see the light of day again. . . .

He managed to scrape into the cage just before the bar was put in place, and his stomach floated away from him during the ascent as it did when the cage descended. He had a constant fear while in the cage of something going wrong and it sticking and them all left huddled here on their hunkers for hours and hours; he was told it happened.

When he stepped out into the daylight there was a light drizzle falling and he lifted his face to it as if in gratitude.

As it was pay day, and although he had only been down a week Big Mullen had told him he would get his wage and then nothing for another fortnight. And so he made his way to where a group of men were gathered round the butty and all arguing; Tom Fitzsimmons was to the forefront and he was holding out his palm on which there was some silver and saying, 'Now look, I'm not standin' for it; thirty shillings I've worked for and thirty shillings I want.'

There were murmurs all round him as men looked at the money in their palms. Then Dick Macintyre, the butty, said, 'The keeker docked me when I sent your skips up, said there was three of your lot half stone; he threw the whole lot out.'

'Threw the whole lot out!' said Tom Fitzsimmons scornfully. 'Aye, and into the owner's pocket; but cut a slice off for himself aforehand. There was no slate or stone in our corves.'

'No, no, there wasn't.' Voices came from different parts of the crowd and Sandy recognised them as those of Jimmy Tyler, Chris Suggett and Fred Jamieson, the men he had been working with all the week.

'Twenty-five's your lot and twenty-five's what you're gettin',' said the butty now. 'Who's next? John Felton, twenty-seven shillings; Mike Casey, twenty-four.' And at this a deep Irish voice now let out a string of oaths.

'Harry Mullen, twenty-five.'

Big Mullen now stepped forward and when the butty handed him his wages he spat on the ground, then turning to the crowd, he demanded, 'Are we goin' to put up with this? We might as well stay up top and starve.'

'Aye. Aye.' There were cries of assent now.

'Somethin's got to be done an' quick. . . .'

'Aye, it has.' It was the voice of Tom Fitzsimmons. 'We'll send a deputation to the manager. . . .'

Now Big Mullen spat in the direction of Tom and said scornfully, 'Manager!' Then again, 'Manager! See the Manager! What good will you get out of that? We've seen the Manager dozens of times; it's the owner we want to see, him in his mansion, stuffing his belly an' that of his friends, banquets and parties, games on the lawns, balls, carried to bed at four in the mornin' and not rousin' again till night. That's who we want to see, THE OWNER. What do you say?' He swung his head round to the crowd, and again there were voices raised agreeing with him.

Tom Fitzsimmons now stepped in front of the men and, his voice grim but controlled, he said, 'You can't get at the owner, you know that as well as me. It's the top manager who'll have to carry our word. And you'll get nowhere by using violence, you know that an' all. Remember what happened in Durham two years back. And again in Jarrow. Lift your hand and you're out of your homes; your bits and pieces on the road, together with your wife and bairns. An' your brains knocked out by the militia. Then they'll bring the Irish in. They've done it afore and they'll do it again. We've got to talk, negotiate, talk . . . talk as well as they do.'

'Talk! Don't be so . . . daft, man.' Big Mullen interspersed his words with a string of curses and Tom Fitzsimmons turned on him a long, cold and penetrating glance, then said, 'If they follow you, Mullen, they won't only end up living on the bare fells, it'll be in the boat to Australia they'll find themselves.' Then addressing the crowd again, he cried, 'And you that have sense know this. Go steady, I say. Jim Tyler there, Chris Suggett, Fred Jamieson and me will go as a deputation to the manager and aye, we'll ask him if we can meet the owner, though that isn't likely. But the time for bonding is only two months off; they'll more likely listen to us now, 'cos they want us to renew our contracts. I say to you, leave it in our hands as you did afore.'

'And where did that get us?' John Felton, Big Mullen's

pal, shouted out now. 'We struck for six weeks and we went back in the same's we come out, except that our ribs were nearly meeting 'cos we had pulled our belts in so tight.'

'You didn't go back the same as you came out,' shouted Tom Fitzsimmons now; 'we've got pumps in A and E sections, and they test now for gas, where they didn't afore. . . .'

'Once in a blue moon,' came a voice from the crowd.

'Well, we haven't had an accident in the last two years.' Tom Fitzsimmons answered the voice; and after this there was a silence until the butty shouted, 'I'm not goin' to stay here all day, there's another half-a-dozen pays.' He began calling names again: 'Putter, Fred Beecham, five and sixpence; Dixie, five shillings; Sandy Gillespie, six and six. . . .'

Tom Fitzsimmons's voice broke in on the butty now, saying, 'The lad should have seven and nine, he was on the face along o' me.'

'He's been docked like the rest of you. There it is, six and six, take it or leave it.'

Sandy took the six and six and looked up at Tom Fitzsimmons, and Tom said quietly, 'It's a bad week, lad. It won't always be like this.'

Sandy nodded at him, then turned away and joined the men walking out of the pit yard, and as he went he thought he would have made as much in the fields and been in God's open air. . . . but then he wouldn't have seen The Nipper.

At the gates Big Mullen passed him with three of his cronies and didn't look towards him. There was no sign of Stan, or Joe or Billy Mullen, and so Sandy, his feet lifting heavily, made his way home across the fells by a short cut that Stan had shown him. This way almost

70

halved the journey but the going was rough and over hilly land, in most part barren of grass and desolate looking. Stan had advised him to keep to the path for there were a series of holes, air shafts, he called them, that led to the disused mine.

This particular mine had been flooded some years ago and had drowned forty-five men and boys in the process. The water rose so high they couldn't pump it out, but Stan had said there were one or two of the top galleries still dry. Stan had also said there was a warren of caves in the hillside, and when he had asked him if he'd been in them he had shaken his head and answered, 'No, not right in.' He had hesitated for a moment before adding, 'And if I was you I wouldn't try either because Mad Mark makes his home in one or other of them, and he'd be just as likely to brain you with his hook if he thought you were nosy.

Sandy had laughed at this and told Stan he needn't worry, for he wasn't likely to go poking into any caves, not after spending twelve hours down one.

He was rounding the foot of a hill just before he came to the slag heap at the mouth of the open cast mine, when he thought he heard someone calling. He stopped and listened, then moved on. And then it came again, and he heard it plainly now, a voice calling softly, 'Mark! Mark! Are ya in there? Come on out a minute.'

Sandy stopped and pressed himself against a boulder He knew that voice, it was Big Mullen's.

'I just want a word with you, man; an' I've got somethin' for you, a drop of the hard stuff. Listen; hear the bottle?' There came the sound as if a knife was being knocked against glass.

'He's not in there.' It was another voice, and Big Mullen answered, 'He's bound to be round here somewhere, and if anythin' will bring him out it'll be the whisky.'

Footsteps were moving towards him now. They seemed to be just at the other side of the boulder and as they came nearer he crept slowly round it. He now recognized Mike Casey's voice, saying, 'Let's try the caves, an' if we get him in the open we'll knock it out of him.'

'We'll get him full first,' said Big Mullen. 'He can't go on resistin' it, and it'll be easier that way. If only we could pin him down.' He swore again.

'Aye, as you say, if only we could pin him down.' This was Peter Armstrong speaking, the man who had bet Sandy that he couldn't approach The Nipper.

When they moved out of sight and sound Sandy slipped round the boulder, then began to run, and when he came to the slag heap and to where the open ground dropped steeply into the mine he ran straight into Mad Mark.

The shock of the impact caught at his breath and nearly choked him, and the hook that dug into his shoulder brought him over sideways with the pain. The hairy face was hanging over him, bright burning eyes staring out of it. He knew that the mouth was moving behind the whiskers but he couldn't see the lips.

Slowly he watched the look in the eyes change and he felt the grip on his shoulder slacken as the old man recognized him beneath the coal dust, and now he gulped in his throat and muttered quickly, 'You'd ... you'd better hide, they're looking for you.'

'Aye ... aye ... they're lookin' for me.' The words were slow and deep, and the voice had a rich tone to it, not like what one would expect from a madman; and it went on, 'They'll not find me though, they'll not find me unless I want.'

Sandy was about to speak when he saw the old man

throw up his head and listen. Then before he knew what was happening his arm was grabbed again and he was being run towards the mouth of the mine. They had no sooner gone into the darkness than he heard the voices of the men and Big Mullen saying, 'John and me'll go in, you keep on the high ground facing the caves; if he's got a bolt hole through he'll come out of one of 'em.'

Sandy's body was one big protest now, but in spite of what he felt, he was powerless, for he was being dragged down an incline and into pitch blackness. When he was pulled sharply to the left and the hook hand dragged him downwards he knew he was going through an air door, and from then on he realized he was travelling upwards. When suddenly he was tugged round a double bend he felt he was glimpsing heaven for there, shining down from above, was a ray of light.

The old man stopped under the air shaft and peered at him and, his voice low, he said, 'It's all right, lad, I'm not goin' to hurt thee. You're a good lad.' He nodded at him, and although Sandy couldn't see the expression in his eyes he thought, from the movement of the hairy face, that the old man was smiling, and when he went on as if they were sitting on the fells talking about ordinary things, 'You caught any rabbits of late?' Sandy shook his head and whispered, 'No.'

'I'll get you one the morrow. You come back the morrow, an' I'll get you one.'

'Aye . . . aye.' During the past minutes he had thought he would never see the morrow, never get out of here alive, and now it came to him again that this old man wasn't really mad, at least not all the time. He watched him put his head to one side and listen; then he brought his face close to his own and asked softly, 'Do you like

Big Mullen?' And without hesitation Sandy replied flatly, 'No.'

'Good.' The old man nodded his head at him. 'He's a wrong 'un. Come on, we'll lead them a dance, eh?'

Sandy had no other option but to follow; and now it was he who held on to Mark's tattered coat, and when they moved into blackness again his ears began to sing, like they did when he went under water in the river. But they weren't under water here, he guessed they were moving up into the hillside.

On and on they went until he lost count of time. He didn't know how long they had been walking. Deep blackness was deceptive; it could have been ten minutes or twenty. And then a wave of relief swept over him as he saw ahead a faint chink of light. It looked long and thin, and when he came up to it he saw it was a cleft in the rock, not more than six inches wide and about eight feet high. As he looked upwards the light disappeared, thinning away, and he knew he wasn't in the pit any more but in a fissure in the hillside, part of one of the caves, he thought.

Now old Mark was saying, 'Follow me. Stick your foot where I do, and grip on to the opening, like this.' He demonstrated with his hook and his hand, and in amazement Sandy watched him stick his foot in a small cleft, grab the inside of the ledge with the hook, then hoist the end of the crutch into a niche with his one hand. He made four such movements and then he was above the light and seemed to disappear into the rock. But his voice came down to Sandy, saying, 'Come on now.' And Sandy lumbered up the wall after him, all the while wondering at the old man's agility, especially with his handicap and his frail-looking body.

When he was above the light a hand came out and

pulled him on to a shelf, then drew him to the further edge of it, before letting go of him, and he watched the old man squeeze through a narrow horizontal cleft, then drop down into a cave about fifteen feet wide and twice as long. And he followed him into what was apparently the old man's home.

In the light that came from two directions, one from a green glow about four foot high from floor level, and which Sandy recognized as light coming through bracken, and the other from a fissure that ran across the top of the high rock roof, he saw in the far corner a bed of grass and dried bracken, an assortment of old clothes, and the remnants of a fire, beside which were an old pan and a tin can.

'There.' The old man flung his hooked arm wide. 'You like it?'

Sandy nodded.

'Tell you somethin'.' Old Mark's face came close to his. 'You're the first body that's seen it.'

'Oh!' Sandy nodded again. 'Ta. Thanks.' His legs were trembling and he wanted to sit down; he was also longing for a drink, and as if the old man had read his thoughts he said, 'Got any tea on you?'

Sandy again shook his head.

'I'd like a drink of tea.' He began to move around the cave as if looking for something, and Sandy said, 'I . . . I could bring you a bit the morrow.'

'Aye, you could. You got a big family?'

'No, only me and me ma.'

'No da?'

'No; he died.'

'Does . . . does your ma bake?' The face was close to his again.

'Aye, usually on a Sunday mornin'.'

'Could you bring me a bit of stotty cake?'

'Aye, I could.' Sandy smiled at him now.

'I'll get you a rabbit for some stotty cake.'

'Oh, I don't want anything in return; what I mean is I'll bring you some tea and bread the morrow with or without the rabbit.'

The old man stared at him. Then Sandy almost cried aloud in protest as once again his shoulder was grabbed and the old man was dragging him to the far end of the cave and to where his bed lay and, thumping it with his crutch, he looked at Sandy and said, 'The morrow, when . . . when you bring me the bread I'll show you . . I'll . . . I'll show you what they're after, eh? The passage. . . . The passage.'

'Thanks,' said Sandy, not knowing what to answer at this moment.

'Nobody knows but me. But you're a good lad; you stopped them peltin' me, didn't you? You're a good lad.' He now patted Sandy's shoulder gently and in a most sensible way he said 'Well, you'll be wantin' to get home; your ma'll be wonderin'. Aye, she will. Well, come on then, I'll show you out. You can't get out that way.' He pointed to the way they had entered the cave. 'See, the wall slopes too far back, can't reach the slit from this side.' He went forward, then stopped and said, 'What time the morrow?'

'Around two o'clock.' Sandy paused. 'It's a safe time; not so many folks about then, I mean takin' strolls.'

'Aye. Aye.' The eyes shone out from the hair with a merry glint. 'Not so many folks takin' strolls. You're a wise lad; you're wise. . . . Can you fetch candles?'

'Candles?'

'Aye, candles. Aye; we'll need candles, three, four.'

'I'll try.'

'Aye, well do that. Come on.'

When they reached the place where the light glowed green the old man got down on all fours and motioned Sandy to do the same, and he crawled after him through a tunnel of bracken and bramble; and when the old man rose to his feet Sandy followed suit, and there, opposite them, was a boulder and the old man whispered, 'I'll be here the morrow. And you'll bring the bread?'

'Aye, I won't forget,' Sandy said, but before he could ask, 'But where's here?' the old man had dropped noiselessly into the bracken and disappeared, and he walked round the boulder and stood gaping. He was standing on the edge of the main road by which they had travelled from the farm the day they had come to Ballast Row. He had come up the other side of the hamlet and only ten minutes walk from home, which was a good thing, for his mother would be worrying about him being late, and he doubted if she would believe his story when he told her. . . .

And he was right, his mother didn't believe it, not at first anyway.

'What do you mean, boy?' she said. 'You went through the old mine and came up yon side of the Row? That mine's been flooded for years.'

'But I'm here, aren't I?'

'Now, don't you be cheeky.'

'I'm not being cheeky, Ma; but I tell you we travelled through galleries, and he brought me up at yon side, a good two miles from the mouth.'

Norah Gillespie stared at her son, then said, 'You shouldn't have gone with him. I tell you, you'll land up in trouble.'

'Aw, Ma, I ask you. Someone grabs you by the arm and pulls you into black darkness, where you can't see your finger afore your face, what would you do?'

Her head wagged as she said, 'He's an old crippled man, you could have pushed him off.'

'Old crippled man, huh! You want to see him, he's like a squirrel, that crutch is a third leg.'

Her head still wagging, but slower now, she said, 'And about the morrow, you're still goin'?'

'If you'll give me the bread and the tea, and a few candles, aye.'

Her whole body became still now as she asked, 'What if you never get out of that passage that he's on about? If he's the only one that knows about it, nobody will be able to find it, or you.'

His voice was soothing as he said, 'If he shows me the way in, Ma, I'll find me way out.'

She turned from him as she muttered, 'Oh, boy, you worry me.'....

And she said the same thing at one o'clock the next day when she wrapped up the fresh steaming oven bottom cake in a piece of unbleached linen, then taking a piece of old paper and twisting it into a cone-shaped bag scooped six teaspoonfuls of tea from the caddy into it. Finally, she paused for a moment with the spoon over the sugar basin. It wasn't every day of the week they had sugar for themselves – she had bought a half-pound yesterday and to spend fourpence-ha'penny on a half-pound of sugar was a luxury. Then with an impatient thrust she scooped three teaspoonfuls into the bag and, pushing it across the table to where Sandy stood grinning at her now, she said, 'There! and get yourself away afore I change me mind and lock you in. But better still get yourself back here and long afore dark, mind, if you don't want me worried out of me wits.'

'I will, Ma. And ... and the candles?'

'Aw!' She went to the cupboard and pulled out four tallow candles from a bundle of twelve. As she threw them on the table she exclaimed, 'Why didn't you take him your wages?'

His grin was wide as he answered, 'I never thought of that, but it's an idea. He looks more in need than us.'

'Get away with you!' She flapped her hand towards him, but when he had reached the door her voice halted him as she said, 'Be careful, boy,' and he answered, his face straight now, 'Don't worry, Ma, I'll be careful.'

He went out the back way as he didn't want to meet up with any of the Mullens, particularly as he was carrying the linen-wrapped parcel and the tops of the candles were sticking out of his pocket. He clambered over the embankment that hemmed in the back of the Row like a fortification; the mound was grass-covered but the ashes, the rubbish and the filth left by the residents of the Row showed through here and there like dirty scabs along its length.

Once over the embankment he began to run, keeping clear of the road until he was near the boulder, and when he came within a few yards of it he stopped. His heart was racing, not only from exertion but with excitement. He walked now with slow steps towards the boulder, went around it, and there, sitting with his back to it, his legs stretched out, was the old man.

At first Sandy thought he was asleep, and stood still; then within the deep sockets of hair the lids were raised and the pale eyes were looking at him, and the hair rippled on the face and Sandy knew he was smiling.

'Afore your time.' The old man looked up at the sun and Sandy nodded, then said, 'I ran.'

'I used to run.'

Sandy said nothing to this but watched him turn on

79

to his knees and swing himself to his foot with the aid of the crutch, then walk round the boulder and to the edge of the road, where he turned his head and, looking at Sandy, said, 'Anybody know you were comin'?'

'Only me ma.'

He now hobbled back towards Sandy and his gaze dropped to the parcel in his hand and he stared at it.

Holding it out, Sandy said, 'It's still hot.' At this Old Mark put out the arm with the hook attached to the end and, allowing his ragged sleeve to drop back, he put his wrist on the linen, then nodded.

Swiftly now he turned about, went down on to his knees and disappeared into the bracken, and Sandy, after a moment's pause, scrambled after him.

In the cave a wood fire was burning between two bricks, and standing on the bricks was a pan of simmering water. Sandy took the tea and sugar from his pocket and handed it to the old man, who made no comment, but after sitting down near the fire opened the bag and looked into it, then sprinkled a third of the contents into the bubbling water. Now he reached his arm up for the warm loaf and held it on his knee for some moments before he opened it; then slowly, as if he was savouring some great delicacy, he broke off a chunk of the bread and began to chew on it, and rhythmically the hair on his face moved up and down as if to a beat. After he had swallowed some mouthfuls he turned to Sandy and nodded his head once.

While Sandy sat silent, the old man ate half the bread, and when he poured the tea into the only mug he possessed and handed it to him first, Sandy shook his head and said, 'Ta, but I've just had me dinner and I'm not all that fond of tea.' Which was a lie.

The pan held three mugsful of tea and when Old Mark

had finished it all he looked at the tea leaves in the bottom of the pan, poured more water on them, and set the pan back on the fire to stew; then heaving a sigh as if he had enjoyed a wonderful meal, he said, 'Well now!' and nothing more.

Sandy waited, and all the while the old man was staring at him. Then again he said 'Well now!' But this time he added, 'What about it?' and Sandy answered 'It's up to you.'

There was another silence; then with a characteristic movement of turning his body around as if to crawl but, instead, bringing himself upright Old Mark said, 'Light your candle.' And Sandy took one of the candles from his pocket and lit it at the fire, then turned to see the old man hobbling towards the far corner of the cave and his bed. He followed, and watched him rake his entire bed of dried bracken and hay to one side with his hook, to expose nothing that Sandy could see but the uneven slabs of rock that formed the floor near the wall of the cave. But it was from this moment onwards that his eyes widened and stayed wide for the next three hours.

The old man now poked the end of his rough crutch into what looked like a slight natural hollow in the rock wall about four foot from the floor. The hollow wasn't as big as an ordinary saucer and it looked one with the rest of the rock until it fell backwards under the pressure of the crutch. Then Sandy's eyes were switched from it as the old man suddenly said, 'Back a bit!' and he jumped back, almost toppling on to the bracken as he did so, for there at his feet, as if it was made of wood, a slab of rock was tilting slowly downwards as easy, Sandy thought, as the trap door in the loft above the stables at the farm.

Now he watched the old man sit on the edge of the hole

and slide out of sight and it was some seconds later when his voice brought him as if out of a dream, saying, 'Well, come on,' and he, too, sat on the edge of the slab, the candle trembling in his hand, and allowed himself to slide into the unknown.

The drop was surprisingly short, in fact it wasn't a drop at all, for he felt his feet touching the ground before his shoulders left the stone, but he rocked unsteadily before he got his balance. Then, the candle raised high, he looked about him.

Old Mark was pulling on an iron lever and Sandy watched the stone slip back into place. He now saw that they were in a narrow roadway not unlike the main one in the mine, only it was more than head high; but unlike that down the mine, the air here was pleasantly cool.

'Frightened?' The word was rapped at him, and Sandy gulped before he answered, 'No, no; I'm not frightened.'

He thought the old man chuckled, but he wasn't sure for his hair distorted the sounds that he made.

He was following him along the passage now holding the candle high. It was impossible to know in which direction the passage led for it twisted and turned every fifty yards or so, and the further he went the more he realized that whoever had hewn the passage out had known about mining, for the roof was held up with huge beams supported on pit props. When, as Sandy imagined, they must have travelled all of two miles, the pit props were suddenly no longer needed, they were walking through a natural crevasse of rock. The old man stopped and looked upwards. Sandy's eyes followed, and there at a great distance above their heads was daylight, but diffused, for the rock walls almost met in places, and the effect was like looking through a window of small panes, some dim with dirt.

The cleft ran for some forty feet and its end was only wide enough for them to ease through sideways; and now they were in another cave. Sandy gazed about him in amazement for the walls were composed of shelves of slate lying in layers and sticking out here and there like counters in a shop. It reminded him of a drapery shop he had seen in Newcastle on his one and only visit there. His da had taken him in to buy thread, and he had seen the bales of cloth piled high up to the ceiling on shelves not unlike these.

The old man sat down now and, pulling the remainder of the bread from his pocket, he began to munch at it, still slowly, still savouring the taste. Sandy thankfully sat down beside him, and as he did so he asked tentatively, 'Is . . . is this the end?'

'End?' Now the old man did laugh. 'Hardly beginnin', lad. Hardly beginnin'. You tired?'

'No, no!' Sandy's answer was emphatic.

After a few minutes Old Mark said, 'Way's different after this, rougher. Come on.'

He was now leading the way through another narrow aperture in the far side of the cave wall, and after emerging they hadn't taken a dozen steps when Sandy stopped and looked at a blocked-up entrance that put him in mind of similar ones he had seen down the mine. Old Mark had stopped too, and as if reading his thoughts he said, 'Dead men ahind there, thirty-seven of 'em. Used to lead into the Balfour mine. That's the way they used to escape from the house. After the explosion they must have started digging straight on, then they came up against that.' He thumbed back to the narrow crevasse in the rock. 'Bad luck if they hadn't. Bad luck if the cracks hadn't been there.'

The old man moved on once again, and Sandy, following, found that his prediction had been right, the going wasn't so good, for he tripped a number of times and almost fell. There were no pit props here holding up the roof; the tunnel seemed to have been hewn out of the solid rock itself, and in places was not more than four foot high; the air, too, was different, like that down the mine, sweat making. At one stage he was on his hands and knees crawling over a floor of jagged slate. He didn't know how far they had come, three, four miles? He was feeling tired, and although he wouldn't admit it to himself his excitement was giving place to nervousness. What if his mother was right and he would never get out of here. What if the old man, knowing some other way out, deliberately left him? Don't be daft, he chastised himself, he'd always find his own way back even in the dark, by groping. And anyway, he trusted the old man.

Again, as if Old Mark had read his thoughts he turned his stooped body and asked, 'Nearly had enough?'

'It's a long way.'

A few minutes later they were walking upright again, but they hadn't taken more than a dozen steps when illuminated in the candle light, which was almost to its end now, Sandy saw facing him the unmistakable shape of a chimney breast, and gazing about him he realized he was in a kind of rough room, not square, not round, which had once been boarded with wood, but now the wood had, in parts, rotted away.

The old man was holding up his hook in warning for quiet. Then creeping forward on his hands and knees he pushed his face against a wooden panel to the side of the chimney breast, and he kept it there for a few moments before turning and beckoning Sandy to him. Moving aside now, he indicated that Sandy should kneel and put his face to the wood at the point where his hook rested near what looked like two knot holes. He did so, and then the candle almost dropped from his grasp.

He was looking down what appeared to be two long tubes, and at the end of them he could see a man, a finely dressed man, sitting at the head of a table; at one side of him was a woman and on the other side was a girl. He could see the elbow of another person moving up and down as the hand transferred food to its mouth. Then his vision was obscured by the figure of a lackey as he moved round the table, a silver dish in his hand.

Like one in a dream, Sandy turned his eyes from the holes and looked into those of the old man, and the head nodded at him quickly as if to say, 'It's true, it's true, you're not dreaming.' Then again warning caution, he took him by the arm and drew him backwards to the wall opposite the chimney breast, and there, going on to his knees once more, he thrust his head and shoulders into a square hole and beckoned Sandy to do the same. Why? Sandy didn't know, for he could see nothing, but a moment later the reason came to him. When the aroma of cooking food assailed his nostrils he knew that this second hidey hole, although on the level with the dining-room was partly above the kitchen quarters, wedged in as it were between the kitchen ceiling and the floor above.

The old man now tugged him backwards, then silently led the way out of the room and along the tunnel again; and he didn't stop once until they had squeezed through the narrow cleft and into the slate cave. There, dropping down with a plop and a deep outpouring of breath, he said what seemed to be his usual phrase, 'Well now!' and Sandy, falling on to his knees and leaning towards him, asked with suppressed excitement, 'Where is it? I mean that house?'

'You don't know?'

'No.'

'Nor would you guess in a month of Sundays. The Manor, Hursthill Manor, and that was His Lordship.' The title was but a form of sarcasm. 'Stockwell, the great, great-I-am.' The old head moved from side to side and the movement held utter disparagement.

Hursthill Manor! Sandy sat back on his hunkers. Hursthill Manor. It was unbelievable. Now again he was leaning forward. 'How ... how did you come across it?'

'Aw.' The old man head's bobbed up and down again now. Then seeming to change the subject entirely, he bent towards Sandy, saying, 'They think I'm mad you know; everybody thinks I'm mad.' He waited for comment but Sandy said nothing, and then the old man, his head lowered, said, 'An' I suppose I do go mad when I get the hard stuff in me. It was on such a night that I found it, the trap door. It was black dark. I hadn't a light, nothin'.' He now stopped and pointed to the candle where the flame was almost touching Sandy's fingers, and said, 'Look slippy, and light t'other, else we'll be in the dark all right.'

'Oh aye.' Sandy quickly lit another candle; then holding it in his joined hands pressed between his knees, he waited and Old Mark began to chuckle. He chuckled a number of times before he went on, 'By! that night, I did get a gliff. I stumbled into the cave. The fire was out, not a glimmer, so I made me way to the corner to lie down, an' there I tripped, just tripped, an' I stuck out me crutch.' He patted the bit of rough wood. 'I thrust it against the wall to steady meself, an' then' – his body was now shaking with suppressed laughter – 'I thought I was going down into hell for the earth was slipping away from underneath me, an' down, down I went, and fear swept over me 'cos, you know, I'd been in hell once.

Nine whole days in hell I was behind a fall in the pit; seven of us there was an' only me left alive. They died, one after the other, and there they were. . . .' He pointed to different spots on the cave floor as if seeing the bodies lying there. 'An' when they got me out I was wrong in the head. Oh aye; they were right then, for indeed I was wrong in the head. An' I don't remember them gettin' me out. I didn't remember anything for weeks after, but gradually I came to me senses. But I was never the same; I couldn't go down again. And when a man doesn't work he becomes hungry, and being hungry I went after a bird on the great Sir William Comb Stockwell's estate, an' Sir William Comb Stockwell had set a nice gin trap specially for me, a man-sized gin trap, an' it whipped them both off.' He lifted up his half leg and his handless arm. 'An' he was for sending me along the line, but then in his mercy—' There was a sneer in his voice now, and he repeated, 'An' in his mercy he said that my punishment fitted the crime. Do you know what his very words were, boy?' The old man was leaning forward now, deep bitterness in his voice. 'That in losing me limbs I had paid me debt to society. Those were his very words, I had paid me debt to society. I didn't know what he meant at the time, but now I do.'

He leant back against the rock and became quiet; and it was as if he had forgotten that they were in a cave deep in the hills, he had gone back to the time when he had been told that he had paid his debt to society.

When the silence had gone on for longer than Sandy could bear and he thought that the old man must have dropped asleep, he prompted softly, 'How did you get out of the hole . . . I mean the trap door?'

'Aw, that!' He was sitting up straight again. 'I didn't . . . I didn't until the day came. I lay there, thinkin' I was in hell. An' then the drink eased me off to sleep an' when I woke I only remembered bits of what had happened, but I was still filled with fright. Then lookin' upwards, I saw the slopin' rock and it all came back to me. It took a deal of contriving to get out, but in my groping I came across some used slabs lying against the wall, put there I'd think for the very purpose I used them, steppin' on to reach up to the floor above. Later I went over in me mind what happened and knew that I'd fallen against some spring that had released the slab. An' do you know?' There was laughter in his voice now. 'I was three full days gropin' around afore I came across that cunning spring in the cup in the rock. By! whoever thought of that had a brain.'

'But . . but what was it used for? I mean—' Sandy waved his hand from one end of the cave to the other – 'the tunnel and that room along there?'

'A priest hole.'

'A priest hole?'

'Aye, a priest hole, where they stayed until they could escape. Hursthill Manor goes back long afore the war atween the Catholics and the Protestants. I remember me grannie saying it was always occupied by a Catholic family, that is until recently, for the Stockwells are rich trash who've only come into money this last hundred years or so. They haven't been in the Manor House more than sixty years. Me grannie worked for this one's father, and they weren't mine owners in those days, just had a few little factories.' He pointed to the candle in Sandy's hand. 'A candle factory, a blackin' factory, an' shares in a brewery; it's only the last forty years or so they've sprung up.' The hairs on his face moved upwards as if his nose was wrinkling. 'Trash!' He said again, 'Trash!'

Once more he lapsed into silence and Sandy waited,

his mind working rapidly all the while. One of the questions he was asking himself was why Big Mullen wanted to know the whereabouts of this passage; it was evident he knew of its existence. He said gently now, 'Doesn't anybody else know about the passage?'

'No; I told you.' There was a note of huffiness in the old man's voice now, and Sandy was quick to reassure him, saying, 'What I meant was, do people know there is a passage to the house but haven't been able to find it, only you?'

Old Mark lumbered up and he was hobbling towards the crevasse in the rock before he answered gruffly, 'Like a story it's been, a legend; hundreds of legends about this part. Fells riddled with legends; smugglers' caves, the lot. But this here was no smugglers' hide-out, 'cos there was no sign left on nothin' like that; where baccy or liquor's been stored there's always a smell left.'

When they passed through the crevasse and reached the further passage the old man suddenly turned on Sandy and growled, 'You'll not go blabbin'?'

'No, no, course I won't. I, I swear.'

'I can get me own back on you if you do, mind.'

Sandy felt a tremor of fear pass through him. The eyes, the tone, were different now from those of the man who had been talking earlier, and he sensed the touch of un-balance in the old man, and so he was quick to say sooth-ingly, 'I give you me word, honest.'

'Your ma?'

'Oh, me ma's as close as an oyster. An'...an' if you don't wish I tell her anything, I won't.'

The eyes stared into his in the candlelight. Then with a twist of his body old Mark swung round again and went forward.

When at last they reached the end of the passage the

old man pushed his crutch into a hollow similar to the one in the cave, and Sandy, looking upwards, knew a feeling of boundless relief when he saw the stone sloping slowly down towards him, and more relief still when the old man said, 'Go on up first.'

He did not need a second bidding. Standing on the stones that were a little to the side and below the hole, he reached upwards and gripped the floor of the cave, his fingers falling into a niche that must have been scraped away for such a purpose. When at last he was standing upright and could see the green-patterned daylight coming through the entrance he almost laughed, his relief was so great, and he realized that all the while he had been wandering around those passages down below he had somehow expected the old man to do the dirty on him.

Now he put out his hands and helped him up through the hole, and when the slab was in place and the bracken and straw once more covering it they walked to the fire, and old Mark, sitting down again, poured out the stewed tea. Again he handed the mug to Sandy, and this time, not only because he was afraid to offend him, but because he was terribly thirsty, Sandy took a long drink of the bitter liquid; then thanking him, he said, 'I'll have to be goin'. It must be getting on, me ma'll be worried.'

'Aye.' Old Mark looked up at him; then he said in a tone as sane as any Sandy had heard. 'It's been grand havin' your company; I . . . I get lonesome at times.'

More touched than he would have cared to admit, Sandy gulped audibly, then said, 'I'll pop in now and again if it's all right with you.'

'It'll be all right with me, lad.'

'Ta-rah then.'

'Ta-rah, son. You know your way out. But be careful when you come up out of the grass. Watch out for folk.'

'I will.' Sandy was on his knees and he turned now towards the figure sitting huddled like a bundle of old rags near the fire and he said softly, 'What am I to call you?' It seemed that the old man was a long time in answering; then he said slowly, 'Mark. Just Mark, lad.'

At this Sandy nodded, turned, and crawled through the tunnel of bracken, but paused and listened before emerging into the open. Then getting to his feet, he walked casually round the boulder and on to the road, and slap into Tom Fitzsimmons.

'Why, hello, lad.'

Sandy gulped again and becoming conscious that his clothes were covered with dried grass and seeds, his hands began what must have appeared like an attack on his body, slapping at his arms, his legs, his thighs, until Tom Fitzsimmons laughed and said, 'Been napping in the hay, lad, eh? Ah well—' he jerked his head – 'You're wise. Get all the fesh air you can when you can, and there's nowt like going to sleep on the open fells. You're coming this way?'

For the first time Sandy spoke, 'Aye,' he said; 'I live along the road.'

'What! In Ballast Row?' There was disbelief in the tone, and half shame-facedly Sandy nodded; then he said, 'It's only for a time until me ma can get a place.'

They walked on in silence for some way before Tom asked abruptly, 'You like the pit, lad?'

'No, not much.' Sandy's head was lowered.

'Well—' Tom dunched him on the shoulder with his arm – 'that's nothing to be ashamed of. I'll tell you something.' He bent down. 'Neither do I.' And now they looked into each other's eyes and grinned. Then Tom went on, 'But it's a livin', at least for a time.' He threw his shoulders back and looked up into the sky, saying softly, 'I've made up me mind I'll not be down there all me life, no.' He turned his head and slanted his eyes towards Sandy as he said with deep pride, 'I can read and write you know, lad.'

'You can!' There was awe in Sandy's voice. 'You went to school?'

'No, I never went to school, but I'm goin' now.' His eyes were shining, his face bright and his voice deep with emotion as he said, 'Twice a week I go to the minister's.' And now his voice was a whisper as if imparting a secret that mustn't be passed on. 'And I'm not the only one. Jimmy Tyler you know, and Chris Suggett, they go an' all. Not Fred...Fred Jamieson.' He smiled tolerantly. 'Fred's all brawn and no brain, but he's a good lad. Oh aye, he's a good lad. But mind.' His voice dropped even lower now. 'Don't you let on to anybody 'cos they don't like it back at the pit, I mean us learnin' to read and write. If Mr Swinburne, he's the manager – likely you haven't seen him yet – but now if he was to get to know, it's ten to one we'd be the first to go when work was slack. Aye—' he nodded slowly – 'that's true. And if it got further, to the ears of the owner, Sir Combe Stockwell, well, my, I'd like to bet we'd be shot out of the pit like balls out of a cannon.'

'Just for learnin' to read and write?' Sandy's voice was equally low.

'Just for learnin' to read and write, lad. You see, when you can read and write you can think. I mean clear thinkin', puttin' two and two together, and you can argue and explain matters.' He straightened his shoulders again, then ended, 'What it boils down to is that you can stand face to face with them up top and say "This is wrong and should be righted, an' what I think should be done is this or that."'

92

There was open admiration in Sandy's eyes as he looked up at Tom Fitzsimmons. He was a wonderful man, the most wonderful man he had ever met. Then without stopping to think he heard himself say in a gabbling tone, 'Could . . . could I learn to read an' write? Could I come along with you, Tom? We've got a Bible but I don't know a word of it. Neither does me ma. Aw—' he moved his head slowly – 'just think, if I was ever able to read it.'

They had stopped on the road, and Tom, putting his hand on Sandy's shoulder, looked at him a long while before he said softly, 'You'll read it, lad, an' not afore long either 'cos this is the time to start, when you're young. I'm going on thirty, and I've only been at it a couple of years or so, but it's brought light into me life; even down in the pit I can see light through me reading. Aye, lad, reading is light. Now lad—' he lifted his finger and wagged it at Sandy – 'you be at the toll gate at nine o'clock next Sunday mornin' and you'll go for your first lesson.'

Tom now pulled open one side of his jacket to show a book covered in brown paper sticking out of a pocket. Then with a dramatic gesture he flapped open the other side and there, in a large pocket at the bottom of the coat, was a piece of rough-edged slate. And now, thrusting his hand into the pocket, he drew out a slate pencil and, tapping it against the slate, he said, 'The key to another world, lad, the key to another world.' There was silence again as they walked on but both their steps seemed to have added spring in them.

They didn't speak or stop until they rounded the bend and came in sight of Ballast Row and when they stopped it was only for a second as they took in the scene before them, for there, at the corner of the Row, struggling in the arms of Big Mullen was Norah Gillespie.

Both Sandy and Tom seemed to spring from a standing start at the same instant and they were side by side when they reached the struggling couple. Sandy dived at Big Mullen, his fists flaying at him indiscriminately for a moment before he found himself thrust aside and almost on to his back, only the house wall saving him; the next minute his mother was beside him clinging to him, and they stood watching Tom and Big Mullen battling it out.

Tom was a good head taller than Big Mullen and his arms were longer but Big Mullen had a wild, vicious strength, and what part of Tom he couldn't reach with his fists he aimed to do with his hob-nailed boots. And one such kick caught Tom on the inside of his thigh, and now it seemed that the fight he had been putting on was merely a demonstration of what was to come, for he went for Big Mullen as if his arms and legs had been multiplied. One of the blows, catching the vicious man on the side of the jaw, sent him somersaulting backwards on to the verge of the fell, and there he lay while Tom stood over him panting; then taking his foot he pushed his opponent and Big Mullen opened his eyes slowly, and Tom, stooping, dragged him up by the collar of his coat, and looking into his dirty and bleeding face, he said, 'If you want some more just try it on again;' then thrust him away and, dusting his hands, he went to where Sandy and his mother were still standing against the wall. But he didn't speak; and they all moved slowly up the street.

When they reached their door, Norah Gillespie, looking from the blood on Tom's hands to the cut on his upper lip that was bleeding freely, said, 'Come in a moment, won't you, and get cleaned up?' and Tom answered simply, 'Thanks,' and followed them into the house.

Ten minutes later, after he had staunched the bleeding

and washed his hands, Tom sat at the corner of the table and looked unblinking at Norah Gillespie while she related how she had come to be struggling with Big Mullen.

'I...I was worried.' She looked up towards Sandy, standing at her side with a mug of tea in his hand. 'He hadn't come back, and I thought he could be lost in those caves....' Her voice trailed away as she felt Sandy's foot kick against hers.

'Caves?' said Tom now enquiringly, and Sandy put in quickly, 'I was just lookin' round, I'd heard tell there were caves up there.'

'Yes, there are, lad.' Tom nodded at him. 'But you be careful, you could be lost in there and never be found again. There's lots of tales about the caves up there. Some people take them as fairy tales, but not me. There's two dead mines hereabouts, and their galleries, those that are not under water, lead for miles up into the hills. It's best to give them a wide berth.'

'Aye.' Sandy nodded at him. Then his mother went on, 'Well, as I was sayin', I was worried and I kept going along to the end of the road because...well, I expected you to come that way.' She looked again at Sandy, and the look held chastisement. 'I'd been along four times but I'd never seen any of the Mullens; and then I was just passin' his door when—' her head drooped – 'when he came out and...and he asked me in.' She paused now before ending. 'When I wouldn't go he tried to make me, and then you came on the scene....' She lifted her head now and smiled at Tom and added, 'And I thank you kindly.'

'Oh, that's all right, missis.' Tom jerked his head. 'The lad here would have dealt with him if I hadn't been along, I'm sure of that.'

Norah Gillespie looked up at Sandy with a smile on

her face now as she said, 'Well, there's one thing, he'd have had a very good try.'

There came a silence on the room before she said, 'You live hereabouts, Mr Fitzsimmons?'

'No, missis, not hereabouts; I've a house in Hebburn.'

'Oh.' She nodded her head agreeably. 'And a family?'

At this Tom shifted the peak of his cap slightly to the side, then said softly, 'I've no family, missis; me wife and child went four years back in the cholera.'

'I'm sorry. Oh, I am sorry.'

He nodded his head, then finishing his tea at a gulp, he rose to his feet, saying, 'Well, well, I mustn't keep you.'

When she rose and went to the door with Tom, Sandy followed, and he looked from one to the other when his mother said, 'Thank you for what you did, Mr Fitzsimmons. And if you're passin' any time you'll be welcome to a drop of tea.'

At this Sandy smiled widely, wanting to endorse the invitation, but he had the sense to remain quiet, and when Tom Fitzsimmons said, 'I'll take up that pleasure, Ma'am, any time I'm passin',' a warm feeling crept over him, as if he had suddenly found security. It was a strange feeling, he couldn't really make it out, just that there was a safeness in knowing that Tom Fitzsimmons was going to call by.

Sandy set Tom about half a mile along the road and when they parted they shook hands like men, like equals. Sandy ran all the way back to the house. When he burst in, his mother was sitting at the table slowly sipping at her tea, and she looked up at him and said, 'So that's the Tom Fitzsimmons you talk about?' and he said, 'Aye.' She took another sip of her tea. 'He's a presentable man, and seems nice.' She nodded her head, and again he said, 'Aye.' Then when he smiled down at her with a wide embracing smile her face became straight and her voice sharp and she demanded now, 'Well, what happened to you down in that cave? Let me have it; you've had me worried to death.'

And he let her have it.

Seven

'Look, leave him lad, and I'll see to him; you've done your stint for the day, you must be fagged.'

'Oh, I'm all right, Mr Stock; I'd rather do him if it's all the same with you.'

'Oh, it's all the same with me, lad; less work for me.'

Sandy went on grooming The Nipper as best he could in the narrow box that was his stall, and The Nipper turned his head and nuzzled him from time to time, and made little ninnying sounds which had amused the horse-keeper when he first heard them – they sounded like a cross between a neigh and a sneeze, he had said. But to Sandy they were a special language and he knew that The Nipper was telling him he wasn't happy. How could he be, twelve hours attached to a bogie, then brought into this rude stable? The only good thing now in his life, besides the presence of himself, was his food, which was good but which at times he just picked over – there was no green grass down here.

Sandy straightened his back and looked over the wooden partition and asked the question that had been in his mind for days but which he had been afraid to voice.

'Mr Stock.'

'Aye, lad.'

'What ... what'll happen to them when ... when the strike starts?'

'The ponies, lad?'

'Yes, the ponies.'

'Well, usually if it's not goin' to be a long 'un they stay down but if it is a long 'un they use it for sortin' out.'

'Sortin' out? What d'you mean sortin' out?'

'Well now, like this time, no matter if the strike's short or long they're goin' to change over. You see this lot's pretty old, past it really. There's Bella—' he thumbed down the line of boxes. 'She's so tired she's off her feed. And Sniffy. Well, that leg of his won't hold him up much longer. Cockeye. He could go on for a year or so but in the change he'd go an' all, Mary Ann with him. Paddy The Kick. He's youngish still, he'll stay.'

'Where do they go?'

'Where do they go, lad.' The horsekeeper screwed his eyes up at Sandy as if he was trying to see him through the dim light from the lantern, and then he said softly, 'Well, there's only one place for worn-out pit ponies to go to, lad, and that's the knacker's yard.'

The knacker's yard. The words churned up Sandy's stomach and made him feel sick, but he couldn't stop himself repeating them: The knacker's yard. The knacker's yard. He looked over the line of partitions at the bobbing heads. He had been down the pit only three weeks but he had come to know every one of them, and although he didn't feel towards the others as he did towards The Nipper he still felt for them deeply.

'Ah, don't look like that, lad,' said Nick Stock sympathetically; 'it's got to happen, they've had their time.'

'They . . . they don't leave them up top just for a few days or so?'

'Oh aye, sometimes, it all depends. They never send

99

them off until they've got a new lot in, for it isn't every pony that can be broken in to this kind of work. I've known some of them be up there a month. Nine weeks once; there was a nine weeks' strike in this pit about five years since. Aye, it's a bit of luck for them if they're up top when a strike's on.' And now his voice sank. 'But it's hard lines for everybody else, lad, tightened belts, and wind in the stomach takes a bit of gettin' used to.' He shook his head again. 'It's a sad state of affairs when you come to think on't that as long as the ponies are down here me wife and me can eat. But I'm on next to nothin' when they're up top.' He turned and patted Mary Ann's rump, adding, 'Life's a queer thing. But there, lad—' he came to Sandy – 'I'd get away home if I was you; you can do nothing about it, none of us can. There'll be a strike an' that's that. The only thing I can say I'm glad about is that they're comin' out under Tom Fitzsimmons and not Big Mullen. Tom's in the open but you never know what Big Mullen's up to.' And now he lowered his voice. 'And if I'm not mistaken, him and his crew are brewing a strong brew this time; I pick up bits here and there, an' I piece them together ... they talk in front of me as if I was of no account.' Here he laughed bitterly, coughed, then added, 'But they're not dead yet, their turn will come.' And at this he walked down the line of boxes, hitting each standing post with his fist.

Sandy hurriedly finished The Nipper, then, putting his arm round the pony's neck, he said, 'Good night, lad; see you the morrow.' And the Nipper tossed his head and tried to strain away from his halter, and at this Sandy made a quick exit.

As he went down the road towards the cage he passed the men and boys starting the night shift. He had the cage to himself as he ascended, and as always when he stepped out on to the gantry he took in one long draught of air and swelled his lungs with it to bursting point.

He now went to the lamp house and left his lantern and his tally, and it was after he had passed the main gate and was rounding the slag heap that he heard a voice saying 'Pst! Pst! Sandy,' and he looked round to see Stan Mullen beckoning to him.

'What is it?'

'Over this way,' said Stan; 'I want to talk to you. Keep off the road.'

'But why? What's up?'

'Come on, an' I'll tell you.' Stan hurried forward and Sandy kept up the pace for a while until suddenly he caught Stan by the arm and said, 'Hold on a minute. Look, I don't feel like a race, I'm tired, man. What is it?'

Stan stopped now, wet his lips, then jerked his head before he said, 'Peter Armstrong an' Mike Casey are waitin' for you along the road.'

'For me?' Sandy thumbed his chest.

'But why, what have I done?'

Stan was walking on again but more slowly now. 'You've been seeing Mad Mark, haven't you?'

They were looking at each other now intently, and after a moment Sandy said, 'Aye. What about it? And how did you know anyway?'

'The lads saw you, an' followed you along the road, an' later through the bracken.'

Sandy turned his head away and bit hard on his lip. Three times during the last fortnight he had visited Old Mark, each time taking him bread and tea, and once a can of broth. But he had talked to him only twice for on his third visit the cave was empty and he had left the bread and tea near the dead fire, and the dead embers told him that the old man hadn't been there for some days.

He turned to Stan now, his face hard and his voice angry as he said, 'Well then, your da and his lot have found what they were lookin' for, haven't they, so what do they want with me?'

'That's it,' said Stan softly; 'they haven't. When they went into the cave there was nobody there. They've been at different times, tryin' to nab him, but they've had no luck, an' they think you know where he's to be found. They think he'll come for you 'cos you've been feedin' him.'

'Well they're bettin' on the wrong horse,' said Sandy, ' 'cos I don't know where he is.'

'Me da doesn't believe that.'

'He wouldn't.'

Stan made no retort to this; then after a moment he asked, 'Does he talk to you?'

'Yes, he talks to me.'

Stan's step was slow now and his head drooped as he asked, 'Has he told you about . . . about the passage?'

Sandy made himself look at Stan as he asked, 'What passage?'

'Oh, there's a yarn that there's a way leads out of the old mine into a passage and it comes up under Hursthill Manor.'

'Well, what if there is? Why would they want to get under the Manor?' asked Sandy now, his eyes narrowing.

'I . . . I don't quite know, I only know they mean no good. It's all because of the strike an' bringing the Irish over. Me da . . . well he says they want a pistol, something to hold at the owner's head, so to speak, and findin' the passage to the house seems to be it. I . . . I don't know the rights of it. He . . . he won't tell me, he talks to Joe more than me.' He turned his head to the side. 'He doesn't trust me, an' I don't blame him.'

'I'm . . . I'm sorry, Stan.'

'Oh you needn't be sorry. It's in me own hands; I'm big enough to go off, an' I was thinkin' of it.' He turned his eyes on Sandy. 'I want to work in the open. . . . I dream of the sea, seeing the sky never ending.'

'They tell me it's no easy life, a sailor's. Why don't you think of goin' on the land?'

'Goin' on the land!' said Stan scornfully. 'Ask yourself, would half of us be down the pit if there was decent land jobs?' And Sandy jerked his chin as he said, 'You're right there. But what I was meanin' was, if you're goin' away, you might try for the land in some place else.'

'I've thought of that. I've talked to this one and that but the further you get away from the North the worse the land conditions are. Down in the South they say they're treated no better than the cattle they look after.'

'Aye, I've heard that an' all.'

They were now skirting the base of a hill and Stan pulled Sandy to a stop, then whispered, 'Climb up after me but keep your head down an' I'll show you them.' And when Sandy peered over the crest he saw in the distance the road, bordered on the right side at this point by a group of boulders behind which, crouched and waiting, were the figures of two men.

'They're going to have a long wait the night,' said Stan with a grin.

'They are that,' replied Sandy. 'Thanks to you. But won't they have a go at me the morrow night?'

'Aye, I suppose so. But you can alter your route; you can get home by half a dozen ways.' They slithered down the hill, and when they reached the bottom, Stan said, 'One thing. We mustn't be seen together 'cos me da would twig. An' you'd better not come along to the drift any-more at dinner-time.'

'Aw, but man, I want to see the ponies.'

'You an' your ponies!' Stan screwed up his face, then said flatly, 'Well, if you do come, don't sit along 'o me, an' don't speak to me. If I want you I'll find you. Right?'

As Stan went to move off Sandy put out his hand and said, 'If . . . if your da and them should get hold of Old Mark how will they go about gettin' the information out of him? I mean, he's an old man, will they knock him about?'

'Oh, there'll be no need for that, they'll just fill him up. He likes the hard stuff, but he's no head for it, it sets him clean barmy. It was the drink more than anything that knocked him barmy. His . . . his wife died when he had a bout on him, she fell in the fire. They couldn't prove that he had done it but it happened about six months after he had been trapped in the mine. And he was caught in the gin trap when he was drunk. They say he's only been drunk twice since, but practically the whole county knew of it for he ranged the hills and bellowed like a stag in the rut.'

'Poor old fellow,' said Sandy softly; and Stan repeated, 'Aye, poor old fellow.' Then added, 'An' it'll be poor old fellow if me da and the others get him, 'cos that's what they'll do, they'll stuff him with it, and he'll talk. He'll talk about anythin' and everythin' when he's full.'

Sandy looked hard at Stan for a moment before he said, 'Well, we'll just have to do our best to see that your da doesn't meet up with him, won't we?' And at this Stan sighed and said, 'Aye, but it's going to take us all our time. An' there's another thing you'll have to watch.' His chin drooped on to his chest and he muttered, 'I don't know whether you've twigged it or not, but me da's after your ma.' His head slowly rising now, he asked, 'There's no chance, is there?'

Chance! Big Mullen and his ma? Sandy's jaw moved aggressively at the very thought of such an alliance and he said, 'None in the wide world.' And Stan gave a mirthless laugh and, half turning away, he said, 'If he had been different it could have worked out, couldn't it?' He looked over his shoulder and Sandy, his face softening now, answered 'Aye, Stan; if he had been different it could have worked out.'

He stood for a moment watching Stan walking away, his shoulders hunched up round his neck as if in protection from a blow, and he, too, turned away and went on his road, a sadness weighing heavy on him, not for himself, or because of The Nipper at this moment, but because of Big Mullen's eldest son, whom he liked, while at the same time he hated his father.

The feeling in the mine for the next four days was one of bitterness, tenseness, and suppressed excitement. After each shift there were gatherings at the pit head, some groups being addressed by Big Mullen, others by Tom Fitzsimmons.

It was on the Thursday night that the manager, Mr Swinburn, stood on the steps leading up to the cage platform and, holding up his hand, demanded the men's attention. But he seemed to be addressing only two of them, Tom Fitzsimmons and Big Mullen, when he said, 'You're mad. You know what this will lead to, the loss of your jobs and your homes. If you can't think of your wives and families then. . . .' At this he was interrupted by voices shouting from the crowd, 'That's who we are thinkin' of.' 'We want fair do's.' 'It's a clean sweep we want:

change the butty and the keeker; daylight robbers they are, both of them.'

'They are only doing their job,' Mr Swinburn shouted back.

'Lining their own pockets, and yours an' all, an' the boss's. There's not a man among us hasn't lost three bob to them in the last fortnight. Reckon that up when you're sittin' down to your six-course meal, Mr Swinburn ... Sir.'

The manager became silent for a moment, staring from one face to the other in the crowd; then, bringing his eyes to Tom Fitzsimmons, he said, 'There'll be bloodshed. You know that's what it will lead to?'

'There'll be no bloodshed if we can talk.' Tom's voice was loud, yet calm. 'Let's come face to face with the owner and put it to him. All we want is fair play: no more fines for things not connected with the mine, such as keeping pigs, and trespassing, no dockin' of full corves for one piece of slate or stone, and safety regulations seen to, a new shaft dug for ventilation;' and now his voice took on a bitter note – 'an age limit for bairns before they can go down.'

'You're not asking much,' sneered Mr Swinburn, and Tom, his voice angry now, cried, 'No, we're not, when it's compared with what you and the owners get out of us. ... They say he's home, then arrange it so he can meet a deputation of us. ...'

'Lot of damn good that'll do.' This was the well-known deep, bellowing voice of Big Mullen. 'Remember, lads, what happened when Bill Stacey tried to see the big fellow a few years back? .. Sir William Combe Stockwell had his lackeys throw him down the steps. Do you mind that time? Huh!' He turned his head and spat against the wall. 'Talk! Talk with him, he says.' He thumbed towards

Tom Fitzsimmons. 'When he can get through the cordon of militia they'll bring in!'

There was loud and angry assent from most of the group now and Sandy saw Tom Fitzsimmons lower his head as if he was weighed down by the truth of Big Mullen's statement. For the moment he seemed to have no defence against it.

Mr Swinburn was speaking again, threateningly now, and when he finished he came down the steps and stamped across the yard, the men sullenly making a pathway for him.

It was as Sandy was pushing his way to where Tom Fitzsimmons was standing in the centre of a group of men that he felt his arm gripped. Turning round, he looked into the narrowed hard stare of Big Mullen.

'You're very fond of the Galloways, aren't you, lad?' The words were growled low.

Sandy made no reply, he just stared back into the mean face; and Big Mullen went on, 'Especially the one called The Nipper. Well, things can happen to Galloways as well as to men, you know that, don't you? They can have their fetlocks slit, and other places that aren't pleasant.'

With a jerk Sandy tore his arm from the man's grasp, and through clenched teeth he replied, 'You dare! Just you dare touch him an' I promise you I'll ... I'll have you. Mind, I'm tellin' you. If I've got to wait years I'll have you. An' ... and listen to this.' He now thrust his face into Big Mullen's. 'Whatever you do to The Nipper, I'll do to you.'

'What is it?' It was Tom Fitzsimmons's voice behind him, and Sandy, gulping on his spittle, turned and said, 'Nowt. Nowt.' He was so angry that he had lost all fear of Big Mullen for the moment.

Tom Fitzsimmons and Big Mullen stood looking at each other; then in a deep weighed tone, Tom said, 'Lay off him, Mullen. If you know what's good for you, lay off the lad.' And on this he turned away, and drew Sandy with him and out of the yard.

They had gone some way along the road in silence before Tom asked quietly, 'What is it? What are you afraid of, lad?'

Sandy remained quiet. The anger was still deep within him, but his mind was working rapidly and his reasoning was telling him to confide in this man, tell him everything. He turned and looked at Tom for a long moment before he said, 'I've got something to tell you, but...but I'd rather you keep it to yourself....'

It was almost ten minutes later when Sandy finished giving Tom the details of his journey through the underground passageways to the Manor. They were standing on the open fell looking at each other, and Tom Fitzsimmons was biting hard down on his lip while his head was moving slowly from side to side. Then nodding at Sandy, he said, 'You know, lad, I've heard tell of that passage since I was a nipper meself, but I've never laid much stock by it, 'cos there's so many tales flying around these parts you learn to take them with a pinch of salt. But one thing is sure; there were these priest holes in the big houses, and Hursthill Manor was always held by a Catholic family until recent years.' He was shaking his head again, and he said, 'And you say there are two peepholes into the dining-room?'

'Aye; they're the nostrils of the boar's head, Mark says. And to open the secret panel from the room side you've got to put your fingers up them and press hard, and this releases the lever on the inside. Old Mark went in once, in the dead of night, when the family were away and the servants were sleeping off their drink. They'd been havin' a kaaley.'

'And Big Mullen's breakin' his neck to find out about the passage, an' for no good I'll warrant. Oh aye, for no good. And his hurry is connected with the strike. You can see that, can't you?'

Sandy nodded, then said, 'I've thought about it from all angles. But if he was to get into the house the servants would nab him afore he could face Mr Stockwell.'

'Oh, I don't think it'll be in Big Mullen's mind to face Sir William Stockwell, Sandy.' They were walking on again. 'No, he's not a man that likes to come face to face with authority.'

'I . . . I thought he might go in and smash up the place. But then there'd be such a noise that they'd be on to him in a minute. There's another thing though I thought he might be up to.'

'Aye, what is it, lad?'

'Well, they have a daughter, haven't they? Twelve or so they say she is. I've thought perhaps he had kidnappin' in his mind.'

'Oh no!' Tom's reply was quick now, and he accompanied it with a wagging of his head. 'No, he's not such a fool as to do that, that would be certain death for him and the lot of them, kidnappin'. No, whatever it is he's up to, it's somethin' that isn't going to hurt his own skin. I know Big Mullen, I've known him all me life, the biggest part about him is his voice.'

When they reached the cross-roads and the parting of their ways, Tom said, 'When are you likely to see the old man again?'

'When I go to the cave,' said Sandy; 'but I'm not sure to find him there, not now.'

Tom rubbed his coal-smeared hand around his black

face, then said thoughtfully, 'There's one thing evident. The old man's keeping out of their way for nobody knows better than himself that his secret won't remain a secret very long if he has a skinful in him.' He shook his head. 'A sad life that. And they tell me he was a first-class hewer in his day, none better. Well, lad, I must get off home, I have another two miles afore me. But later on the night, if I'm along this way, I'll.. I'll look in on you.' He inclined his head towards Sandy, and Sandy nodded and said, 'Aye, I'll be seeing you then.'

As Sandy turned away, he thought, it wasn't only himself Tom was coming to see, it was his ma; but the thought did not disturb him. Although there had been moments during the last few weeks when he had felt slight spasms of jealousy, especially when on Sunday morning his mother had risen at five o'clock, as if she had to go to work, and had got through her washing and household chores, then had baked a lardy cake and put currants in it, after which she had gone into the pantry and washed herself thoroughly in a bucket of water and had come out looking fresh and bonny with her hair neatly coiled on the top of her head. It was on that day he had felt jealous, for he had never known her take so much trouble before, at least not since his father died. But at the same time he looked on Tom's visits as a protection for her, and not for her alone, but for himself also.

But what protection had the ponies against Big Mullen? The thought suddenly stabbed his mind and he felt again that awful sickly feeling in the pit of his stomach.

Eight

They went on strike on the Friday night, and as the men gathered outside the main gates to listen to Tom Fitzsimmons who was about to tell them what exactly he and his committee meant to do, they were interrupted by the manager calling from an upstairs window of the pump house. 'Fitzsimmons! Listen to me, and take in every word. You and your crowd make one move towards the Manor House and I'll have the militia on you. Now mark my words. One move and I'll have the militia on you.'

Before the window had banged down, Big Mullen's voice could be heard above the murmurings, shouting, 'There! What did I tell you? Reason he says.' He pointed his black finger up at Tom. 'Reason. He's always yarping on about using reason, an' where's his reason got him? One move towards the Manor and what happens? Does he get the corve business straightened out, or the mine safety seen to, or the time shortened for the bairns he's so worried about? No, he gets nowt but the militia, who would shoot you down as soon as look at you. Reason! Reason, be damned!' He let out a string of oaths, then marched away from the crowd, followed by his cronies.

Those who were left looked at Tom and said, 'You know he's right, man; in the long run, he's right.'

'Try it my way first,' said Tom now. 'Just hold out

my way for a couple of weeks an' see how things go. If I fail, well, then you can say scrap reason. . . . All right?'

'All right.' The words came from here and there in the crowd, accompanied by noddings of the head.

When the men dispersed Sandy made his way hurriedly back into the yard and to the storehouse, where he knew he would find Nick Stock. The horsekeeper was talking to the assistant manager, and Mr Wilson's words came plainly to Sandy's ears, and on the sound of them he felt that his heart was dropping down into his boots, for Mr Wilson was saying, 'Bring up the old ones, they're finished anyway. Put them in the meadow behind the tip.'

'What about the other two, Paddy and the new one, The Nipper?' the storekeeper was asking now, and Mr Wilson replied 'They'll come to no harm down below.'

'Aye, aye, sir, you're right there; they'll come to no harm down below.' There was relief in Nick Stock's voice; as long as there was a pony down below he was sure of his full wages. Then as if the Assistant Manager was reading his mind with regards to money he said, 'But then, what's the good of leaving two down? Bring them all up. By the sound of that lot out there this latest madness could go on for weeks. Yes, bring them all up and they can fend for themselves.'

'They'll need to be watered,' said the horsekeeper tentatively now; and Mr Wilson, pursing his lips, replied, 'Very well, tell the checker you'll go on half time, and that'll include getting the four old ones to the yard mind, to finish them off. But I'll see about that later.' On this he turned and marched out, glancing at Sandy as he did so.

Sandy was breathing heavily as he went slowly up to Nick Stock and said, 'Can . . . can I give you a hand?' and Nick said, 'Aye, lad. I'm goin' to need more than four hands to get that lot up. They're scared stiff of the cage and as likely as not they'll kick our brains out if they're not strung down hard.'

Sandy smiled as he followed the horsekeeper out of the storehouse and towards the ramp that led to the cage gantry, and he thought that there was one Galloway that wouldn't need to be strung down and who wouldn't kick their brains out, and in this moment he found himself thanking God for the strike. What mattered an empty belly as long as the Galloways were up above, and most of all The Nipper?

Nine

'Why don't you come to the fields with me, lad? Here's nine days you've been idling, it does you no good.'

'I've told you, Ma. If I've told you once, I've told you a dozen times, I can't. It would be blacklegging; they'd string me up.'

'Don't be silly, boy.'

'I'm not being silly, Ma.' He came and stood in front of her. 'You don't know them. They're not all like Tom and Chris Suggett and Jimmy Tyler and Fred Jamieson and that lot; no, there's more than enough like Big Mullen and Mike Casey. There's one fellow called John Felton. He walks sideways like this—' he now demonstrated, pulling his shoulder down and drawing his left leg up. 'They say it's because he's worked on his side in eighteen inch seams since he was a bairn. He doesn't often speak with his mouth; it's either with his boot or his fist. Ma, you know nothing about life. . . .'

Norah Gillespie now put her hand over her mouth to suppress her laughter, but her eyes twinkled brightly and she made herself say, 'No, I know nothin' about life, lad.' And Sandy came back at her, crying, 'Aw, you can stop tickling me ribs, it's nowt to laugh at. I meant life down the pit.'

Her face straight now, she said, 'No, you're right, lad,

it's nowt to laugh at. But I was only thinkin' of you and your own good.'

'Well, I'm not wastin' me time, Ma; I keep the house clean, don't I? I get your meals ready and I'm learnin' me letters.' He pointed to the little dresser where, next to the Bible, lay a new piece of slate and a pencil.

'I know all that.' Her voice was sharp again. 'But that doesn't take you all day, the rate you go. You know what I'm gettin' at when I say wasting your time.' She flounced around now, grabbed up her shawl and put it on. Then picking up her bait from the table, she went towards the door and, pulling it open, let in the early dawn light. But now she turned towards him, her face softening as she said, 'Well, whatever you do, lad, be careful.'

'I will, Ma,' he answered her as softly. 'Don't worry your head, I will. . . .'

He had tidied the room, washed the crocks, brought fresh water from the stream, cleared out the ashes and built up the fire, and for an hour or more he forced himself to put his mind to learning his letters. Then he left the house. He left it stealthily, looking first out of the back door and then out of the front, and then out of the back again before making a dash for the ash mound across the lane. When over it he bounded like a hare among the hillocks and boulders, until, approaching a higher hill, he stopped for a moment as he recalled the memory both of last night and the night before when his mother and he had sat up in bed startled by a weird sound, not the uproarious sound of Big Mullen or the cheeky brawling of the two younger ones; no, this sound had been half human, half animal, and it had come from over the hills here. It was like someone wailing from a mountain top.

The night before last his mother had said it could be an animal in pain, a deer, but she'd heard nothin' like it afore. When it happened again last night, she had whispered through the darkness, 'What do you make of it, boy?' and he had replied, 'I don't know, I can't put a name to it.'

And now the wailing sound had, in some strange way, become connected in his mind with Big Mullen and the fact that he hadn't seen him for two days. Yet at the beginning of the week he'd had his work cut out to dodge him. . . .

The Nipper was waiting for him at the gate and he tossed his head several times and gave him a greeting, and Sandy, stroking him, said, 'Watcher, lad. How's it going?' And The Nipper's loud neigh said, 'Wonderful. Wonderful.'

Sandy now snapped a piece off a large crust and gave it to him, and breaking the remainder into five pieces he distributed them among the others. When Paddy The Kick, baring his teeth, scattered them as he came up to Sandy for an extra share, The Nipper turned his back on him, lifted his heels and gave him a taste of his own medicine, and Paddy The Kick went scampering off, leaving The Nipper neighing and nuzzling Sandy as much as to say, 'That's shown him who's boss.'

Sandy laughed at this and put his arms around the Galloway's neck, but even as he laughed he thought, As soon as the strike ends he'll be for down below again. Me an' all. And he sighed and wondered why things had to be like this. . . .

It was around noon, while he was sitting with his back to the stump of a tree eating his dinner bait and watching the ponies munching at the grass, that Stan came across the field towards him, and he greeted him pleasantly, say-

116

ing, 'Hello there.' But Stan merely grunted; then squatting down on his hunkers in front of him, he said flatly, 'They've found the way in.'

Sandy was up on his knees now, his face a few inches from Stan's. 'Old Mark. What's happened to old Mark then?'

'Haven't you heard him these last two nights?'

Sandy screwed up his eyes. 'That wailing noise?'

'Aye, that wailing noise.'

Sandy shook his head slowly, then asked quietly, 'Did they hurt him?'

'No, they didn't need to. It was our Joe who gave them the idea that they were too thick-headed to think of themselves, else they would have had him afore now. "Just leave a couple of bottles," he said, "in the cave and in the front of the mine." An' they did that. It was too much for the old fellow, an' they've kept him drunk ever since. But it wasn't till last night that he showed them the passage. An' you know where it leads?' Stan's voice dropped to a whisper. 'Right through the hills to the Manor House.'

Stan was staring at Sandy, waiting for some exclamation of surprise, and when Sandy said dully, 'I know, I've been along it,' Stan let his body fall slowly backwards on to the grass and repeated in amazement, 'You've-been-along-it?'

'Aye, Old Mark took me.'

'Old Mark!' Stan narrowed his eyes. 'You say he took you along that passage?'

'Aye.' Sandy nodded his head. He felt in some way this news was hurting Stan and he tried to lighten it by saying, 'It was likely because me ma baked him a loaf,' and after a moment of staring Stan seemed to accept the explanation.

Now Sandy asked quickly, 'But what do they mean to do now they've found the way?'

'I don't know.' Stan pressed his lips tight together, then repeated, 'I don't know. But it's nothin' that's going to harm them, I know that, for they're nowt but a lot of cowards.' His head drooped. 'Me da an' all.'

Sandy stared at Stan's bent head for a moment; and then he said with urgency, 'But this is serious, Stan. They must be up to no good, I mean to them up at the Manor, and whatever they do it won't be them alone that will suffer, it'll be everybody in the pit. If they get up to any real bad mischief the militia'll come in, and you know what that means, you've heard it often enough. Can't... can't you do something? Couldn't you go to the disused mine, or to the cave, and pretend... pretend that you want to see him about something? You might twig then what they're up to.'

'I wouldn't dare, he'd brain me. He's threatened what he'll do if he catches me around. He's got the idea I'll split. He's mad. They're all mad when they get the hard stuff in them. And they'll be madder the night 'cos young Bill's just brought six bottles down.'

'Six bottles!' said Sandy on a high note. 'But... but that would cost a pile of money. How do they manage it?'

'Oh.' Stan jerked his chin upwards. 'T'isn't the real stuff, not what you get from the bar, or stuff that's smuggled from France. That kind goes to the shopkeepers, aye an' the parson. No, this is hell liquor that they make up in the hills.' He pointed over a section of fell land to a distant blur on the horizon. 'There's a still up there. Nobody knows exactly where for very long 'cos they keep movin' it, 'cos of the Excise men. Bill has a barrow he gathers wood in, it's got a false bottom.'

Sandy sat back and stared at Stan. The things he had

learned in the last three weeks. Now he knew why Big Mullen could afford to be drunk nearly every night while other men with leanings that way could only manage it on a Saturday night. He bent now towards Stan and said, 'Look, Stan, this is really serious; we've got to do somethin'. If it's only trying to get near the cave. We might hear something. There's a passage through the bracken. They'll know of that now, but the last time I was there I took the lay of the land and the bracken covers the hillside in front of the cave. It's pretty sheer, but I think we could climb it. Anyway, we could try. What do-you-say?'

Stan nodded slowly now, then said, 'Me da and Peter Armstrong are goin' to the sports over Felling way s'afternoon. He wouldn't miss the bull baiting.' He jerked his head at this, and his face took on a sneer as he repeated, 'No, he wouldn't miss the bull baitin'. An' I know he's got a bet on Peter Armstrong's whippet in the rabbit coursing. They should be away all afternoon. But as far as I can gather John Felton and Mike Casey are not going with them, so it's me guess they'll be stayin' in the cave lookin' after the old man, keepin' him drunk that is, 'cos once he sobers up he'll be off an' likely as not give them away. At least that's how I reckon.'

'And I think you're right.' Sandy nodded at him.

'What time is it now?'

They both looked up at the sky. 'About half-past twelve I should say,' answered Sandy, then asked, 'What time is your da likely to leave?'

'Around one, it's an hour's walk.'

'Well, we could set off now, couldn't we?' Sandy got to his feet and Stan said, 'Aye.' Then looking to where the ponies were grazing, he remarked quietly, 'They look different up top, don't they?'

'They feel different an' all,' Sandy answered.

'I wish I had your way with them,' said Stan, regret in his tone now.

'You just need to be kind to them.' And to this Stan said thoughtfully, 'Aye, I suppose so.'

As they were making their way out of the gate there came the sound of galloping hooves behind them and Sandy turned and waited for The Nipper, and when the Galloway brought himself to a stop, as if applying a brake to his hooves, Sandy laughed and said, 'It's all right, man, I'm comin' back.'

Stan now laughed his tentative laugh as he said, 'You know, man, you'd think he knew what you were sayin'.'

'He does.' Sandy paused, then suddenly made up his mind that this was the time to let Stan into his secret. 'Watch this.' He went and stood in front of The Nipper and said, 'Well, how you keepin'?' and when The Nipper lifted its hoof and extended it towards Sandy, Stan's mouth fell into a gape, which caused Sandy to laugh as he gave the next order. 'Down and out,' he said. And when The Nipper lay down and became still until given the order to rise, Stan's eyes were as wide as his mouth and Sandy's laughter was high.

'Sore leg. Aw, boy! you have a sore leg.' When The Nipper had completed a limping circle Stan stood gazing at Sandy and, his voice just above a whisper, he murmured, 'You've done that all in three weeks?'

'No. Two years. Come on.' He went out of the gate and closed it after him, and then, giving a last pat to The Nipper's nose, he added, 'Two full years, a bit every day.'

'What-d'you-mean, two years?' said Stan, walking by his side now but gaping at him all the while.

'Well, you see, Stan, I brought The Nipper up. He

belonged to Farmer Blyth, him I worked for afore he went bust, and ... and when I knew The Nipper was down below, well, that's why I asked your da to get me set on.'

Stan had stopped. His expression was showing utter astonishment. He was silent for a time, then he muttered, 'You're a queer one, you know. I've never met a bloke like you afore. You've got spunk. I've always admired spunk 'cos I've never had much meself.'

'Don't be daft.' Sandy gave him a push with the flat of his hand and laughed. But Stan remained solemn, and continuing where he left off, he said, 'It's true, I haven't any spunk. If I had I would have left our lot years ago. But lately, well, I don't know. Things are changin', I've got a feelin' that things are gona change.' He looked at Sandy, and Sandy at him, then they went on their way in silence.

A quarter of an hour later they were lying in the long grass at the foot of a steep incline, and Sandy, his mouth close to Stan's ear, whispered, 'I'll go first, and if you want me to stop pull on my foot, an' if I want you to stop I'll put me two heels together. That's if I can,' he added, 'for I don't know what I'm goin' to find the ground like under the bracken.'

In the green gloom Stan nodded at him: then Sandy moved forward.

There was a strong fresh breeze blowing, which was a mixed blessing, because whereas the waving fronds would hide their movement through them, where the bracken was sparse the wind was bending the fronds low.

At first the going wasn't too steep, but quite suddenly Sandy was confronted by a slaty outcrop the top of which reared up beyond the bracken. Climbing over it was out of the question for if anyone was on the watch they would be seen instantly, and so he indicated to Stan who was alongside him now that he meant to crawl the length of the jutting ridge.

The ridge soon flattened out to bracken height, but they had to crawl about fifty feet beside it before they could round it and make their way back to what Sandy thought would be the point above which they had started and directly below the cave.

They were climbing steeply now and twice they had to pause and lie spreadeagled, tight against the hillside, while trying to negotiate an open loose-shaled area which was bare of bracken. But after another few minutes, Sandy, who had gone ahead, brought his heels together and dug his toes in and lay still; then slowly he signalled to Stan with a movement of his hand along the ground to come up beside him.

Stan had no sooner obeyed him than they each felt the other start for there, not more than three feet away from them, the ground, levelled out under trampled bracken, revealed the cave mouth and from it there was crawling the figure of a man, and if Sandy had leant forwa·d and stretched out his arm he could have touched him.

They both held their breath when the face lifted upwards and the eyes seemed to look straight into theirs, and they slanted their gaze at each other and let out their breath when, after a moment, they saw him crawl away along the path towards the boulder. But the next minute Sandy was nudging Stan, for there, his head poking out from the cave entrance, was Old Mark, and it was evident that if not absolutely drunk he had been drinking. It also became evident that the old man was going to try to escape for he glanced quickly along the bracken tunnel and was actually dragging himself from the cave mouth with the intent, Sandy thought, of diving straight into the bracken and on to them, when Mike Casey's voice checked him, saying, 'Ah! Ah! old 'un. You would, would you? An' after me bein' kind to you an' all. Now get yersel back in there. Fancy you tryin' to leave me an' three bottles still full. Go on.' He took his fist and pushed the old man roughly and Old Mark whimpered, 'Want air. Want air.'

'Aye, well,' Mike Casey answered, 'sit where you are then. No further, mind; you can get all the air you want there.'

In the moment's silence that followed, Sandy and Stan darted glances at each other. Then Mike Casey's drunken voice came again, saying, 'Now fancy that, you tryin' to diddle off. Why man, I thought you were with us an' wanted to hear the big bang. You said last night you'd like to hear the big bang, didn't you?'

'Dangerous. Dangerous.'

'Aye, it's dangerous, but not for us, old 'un, not for us.'

'Cruel, 'tis cruel.'

'No, old 'un, no. They'll know nowt about it. It'll happen like that, puff!' There was a sound of Mike Casey's palms clapping together, then of his voice laughing as he finished, 'They won't know what hit 'em, nor who hit 'em. Won't be able to pin it on nobody, unless they blame the lackeys, and the divil's cure to that lot. I'd like to see them swingin', the pot-bellied lazy nowts. An' once it's over you can go roamin' again, old 'un, howling your bloomin' head off.'

'When?'

'Aw, now can't tell, can't tell yet. If Big Mullen and Peter get what they're after the day then it could be the

123

night; if not, the morrow night or the next night. But soon, old 'un, soon....No, no! you don't.' Mike Casey grabbed at the old man as he made to scramble forward, and he dragged him backwards into the cave, saying, 'That's the thanks you get for being kind.'

Sandy felt the blood draining from his body; he felt that his face was white, as indeed it was. He also felt sick. Silently, he motioned to Stan to move back; and now they went cautiously until they came to the outcrop, but once they had rounded it they slithered quickly down through the bracken to the foot of the hill. There they sat and looked at each other in silence for a moment, and it was Sandy who at last whispered, 'They're going to blow it up, the Manor?'

Stan nodded his head slowly as he muttered in a dazed way, 'Aye. Aye, that's it.' Then screwing up his eyes tightly, he groaned, 'Oh my God! He'll go along the line, he'll be strung up.'

In this moment Sandy realized that Stan was thinking of no one but his father, and he knew, without fully understanding, that he bore him some affection. But also in this moment he himself would have liked to see Big Mullen strung up, for he intended to murder a houseful of people. They might be rich, and they might oppress the poor – they did, there was no doubt about that – and they were so high and mighty that an ordinary man couldn't get near them, but still they were human beings.

Something must be done. He turned swiftly on to his knees and gripped Stan's arms. 'They'll have to be warned, I mean them at the Manor.'

Stan nodded dumbly; then as if coming out of a dream he was on his feet and saying, 'No, no! man. They'll trap them. They'll all swing. An' others along of them. Alec Bridges; he's in charge of the blasting material, nine bairns he's got and his own mother and father; they'll trace it to him.'

'Well, he shouldn't have gone in with them, he shouldn't be giving them the stuff.'

'Ah, man—' Stan threw his arms wide – 'you don't know me da when he gets his mind set.'

'But, listen, Stan. Think, think what'll happen if they're not warned.'

Stan turned his head as far on to his shoulder as it would go; the conflict of loyalties was tearing at him, he could see the gibbet now. There would be no Botany Bay for his da or any of the others if they were caught. Yet as Mike Casey had said, if the Manor was blown up they couldn't pin it on anybody; they might lay the blame on the miners but they couldn't deport the lot of them. . . . Or could they?

Sandy was now gripping Stan's shoulder, demanding his attention as he said quickly, 'I know a family at the Manor farm, the farmer I used to work for and the daughter, Katie; I . . . I could tell them an' they could pass it on. Will you come with me to bear me out, in case they think I've gone potty? It'll sound like that to them I know.'

Stan turned his head away muttering, 'I can't, man, I can't.'

Sandy stared at him, his lips pressed tight together; then he said, 'Well, go and find Tom Fitzsimmons, or one of his men and. . . .'

'No! No!' Stan swung away. 'That's almost as bad as the militia. They'll murder each other.'

'Aw you!' Sandy's voice and face were full of anger now. 'It's as you said yourself, you've got no spunk, you're gutless.' And with a disparaging flip of his hand he turned from Stan and began to run.

The shortest route to the Manor would be by way of the gibbet milestone, then cutting across the ford. It should be low enough to plodge across now, although at the other side he knew he would be trespassing on private land for nearly a mile, but he'd have to risk that.

When he reached the ford he found the water higher than usual. He guessed it must have been raining up in the hills although they hadn't had any down here. His knee-breeches were wet almost to the thighs when he reached the other side.

He didn't run so quickly through the wood and he kept his eyes fixed on the narrow path all the time looking out for spring wires; for this was where the owner would set his gin traps. He heaved a deep sigh of relief when he came out of the wood and on to open land again, and having gained his second wind he ran as swiftly as he could for the next two miles. But by the end of it his pace was much slower, and when finally he reached the farm he leant against the gate post gasping for breath.

As he stood there looking into the farmyard, it came to him that the place was unusually quiet. Across the road cows were grazing in a field, while away in the distance he could see the small bobbing figures of horse and man ploughing a furrow.

He turned now and hurried into the yard. There was no one to be seen. Apprehensively he went towards the back door of the house and knocked gently, but there was no answer to his knock. Then he was startled by a voice calling from across the yard, 'What you want?'

'I ... I want to see Farmer ... I mean Mr Blyth or Mrs Blyth.'

'Eh?' The man put his hand to his ear and Sandy walked towards him. 'I've come to see Mr Blyth.'

'What's that?'

Now Sandy was shouting into the old man's ear. 'Mr Blyth! Or Mrs Blyth, or Katie!'

The man looked at him puzzled and shook his head; then Sandy swept his arm wide around the yard, taking in the house, indicating its emptiness, and now the man tossed up his head and said, 'All gone to fair, out Felling way, fair day. Master alus takes everybody to the fair on fair day. What you after?'

Sandy went to put his mouth towards the man's ear again, then drew back. What was the good, he'd never be able to make this fellow understand? But there must be someone around besides him. He nodded at the man, then walked away, and when he was out of sight he dodged around by the side of the house, along the front and up the other side and through a gate and into the main road again, and he saw no one. There was still the distant figure of the ploughman on the horizon, but as Sandy knew only too well distances were deceptive. That man could be a couple of miles away and probably didn't even belong to this farm.

He walked now disconsolately along the road by the dry stone wall that bordered the series of small fields, and it was as he stopped at one point and leant against it that he saw in the distance, and beyond another dry stone wall, a great stretch of parkland and coming across it someone driving a gig.

Without stopping to consider he leapt the wall and raced across the field, jumped an irrigation ditch, then further on another. As he came within view of the wall that bordered the parkland, he noted it was high in parts, almost five or six feet, and was footed by a ditch like a miniature moat, which made it inaccessible. But to the far right, across a potato field, the wall appeared broken.

Knowing that if he were caught the penalty could be

a whipping at least, he ran straight across the potato field and found to his relief that the ground here levelled off towards the wall where at one part the top stones had crumbled, or had been knocked off – more likely been knocked off by jumping horses he surmised, for the stones had been laid against the wall, not put back as they should have been. He reckoned that this gap had been left for the less agile hunters.

The gig was nearing the path that skirted the wall now and he was amazed to see that it was being driven by a girl, a girl not as old as Katie. Again without thinking of the consequences he leapt over the broken wall and, standing on the path, stretched his arms wide and flapped them up and down as a signal to the driver to stop. But the pony was almost on him when he realized the girl had no intention of stopping, and as he leapt aside he grabbed at the reins and brought the animal to a dragging halt, its head towards the wall and the little trap at an angle across the road.

As he looked up at the driver he did not take in the fact that she was very pretty, and beautifully dressed, but that while she held the reins in one hand in the other she was holding her whip high above her head, ready to strike. For a moment they stared at each other. Then she cried at him in a thin high voice, 'You dirty creature! Let go of him. How dare you!' The next moment the whip slashed downwards and the thong curled round Sandy's wrist, causing him to cry out and let go of the pony.

As he staggered back against the wall grasping his wrist with his hand he forced himself to ignore the pain and shout at her, 'You must take a message to the house. It's . . . it's goin' to be blown up.' Before he had finished speaking she was turning the pony on to the path again, and it was unlikely that she heard what he said for in a voice that trembled, because she was evidently frightened, she cried, 'I'll have them set the dogs on you.'

He watched her whipping the pony into a gallop straight across the park in the direction in which he could see the chimneys of the house rearing up behind a mass of trees.

Still holding his wrist he went back over the wall, and although he knew that her threat of setting the dogs on him wasn't an idle one he did not run as he crossed the potato field, nor yet when he reached the road. He was tired, despondent and fearful.

When, half a mile along the road, he came abruptly on the main gates of the Manor his spirits rose again and he thought, That's what I'll do, I'll tell the lodgekeeper. He ran towards the gates now and, hanging on to the iron bars, he pulled at the bell as he shouted, 'Hi there! Hi there!'

There was no immediate answer and he thought dolefully, The Fair; he's gone an' all. Then, he saw the lodge door open, and a man came hurrying out, fastening his coat. He had obviously been asleep for he came towards the gate blinking his eyes; then peering down at Sandy, he said, 'What you want?'

'I've . . . I've got something to tell you.'

'Aye; well, whatever you've got to tell me I've got nothin' to give you, so off with you.'

'I don't want anything,' Sandy shouted at the man; and he repeated 'I don't want anythin'; nowt, I just want to tell you, to tell them up there—' he pointed along the drive – 'that they're in danger. The . . . the house is goin' to go up.'

'Oh, the house is goin' to go up, is it? That's what your lot would like. Now get off afore I go and get me gun. And if I was on t'other side of the gate, lad, I'd knock your idea of fun out of you.'

'I'm not funnin'. Don't be so thick skulled... you...' Sandy bowed his head and gripped the bars tighter.

'You, you little scut! Thick-skulled am I?' As the long iron chain attached to the gate came across Sandy's knuckles he jumped back and cried out in pain for the second time within fifteen minutes. As he danced he held his fingers under his arm while the man yelled at him, 'You're gettin' off lightly, so be on your road while you've got a whole skin.'

Water akin to tears was raining down Sandy's face from his smarting eyes and as he backed away he cried grimly, 'You'll be sorry. I'm tellin' you, you'll be sorry.'

When he saw the man make to open the gate he turned and ran with a shambling gait up the road. His left wrist was burning unbearably and across the knuckles of his right hand a dark blue weal was rising. The skin of the middle finger was broken and the blood was seeping slowly from it. People! He shook his head desperately and choked back on the sensation of actually crying. People were awful, awful. No wonder Big Mullen wanted to blow them up, for it wasn't only the rich, like that girl, it was the poor an' all. What was a lodgekeeper after all? Nowt! nowt! yet he treated him as if he were scum. Oh! he groaned, and not from pain now. It was as Tom said, you had to beat them, not with blows but with brains; you had to learn to read and write and count and ... and talk, and argue....

By the time he reached home he felt sick with worry and pain. There was no one in the street, no sign of any of the Mullens, and there was no one in the house. His mother had said she'd be home early today as the work was almost finished on Poulter's Farm. Early could mean six o'clock, and it was nearly that now.

He held his two hands in a bucket of spring water to try to ease the burning pain; then he blew up the fire and brewed himself some tea, after which he set out the mugs and plates for the meal, and put the stewpan, with the remains of last night's meal, on the hob to warm.

He had just sat down to drink his tea when his mother came through the door, and as she took off her cotton shawl she walked slowly towards him, saying, 'What is it, boy?' She was looking at his face, not his hands, for it looked grey, and when her eyes travelled from it to his hands she picked them up and looked at the snake-like weal around one wrist and the bruised and bleeding knuckles on the other, and she whispered, 'What is it, what's happened to you?'

'Sit down, Ma.'

She stared at him a moment longer before gently dropping his hands and pulling the chair forward; and when she was seated, he said, 'There's goin' to be trouble, Ma, great trouble; Big Mullen's plannin' to blow up the house, the Manor.'

He watched her draw back from him and press herself tightly against the uprights of the chair, then cup her face in her hands and shake it slowly before she muttered, 'Oh my God! boy, no!'

He nodded. 'I . . . I've been over there to the farm. I've tried to tell them. They're all at the fair. I saw one man but he was stone deaf, and then—' he paused and his head drooped – 'I saw the young lady from . . . from the House. She was in her go-cart. When . . . when I stopped it she . . . she gave me that.' He held out his wrist, then lifting the other hand he finished, 'And the lodgekeeper gave me this. Nobody would believe me, they wouldn't listen.'

Norah Gillespie was now rocking herself backwards and forwards while she patted her cheek with one hand, saying, 'We must tell the Justice, we must get ourselves into Jarrow and tell the Justice.'

'No, Ma; you'd have to give names, an' you know what would happen then.'

They stared at each other. Yes, she knew what would happen then. She had seen a man gibbeted when she was a little girl; her granda had taken her to see him. It was a sort of treat, but she'd had nightmares for years afterwards. She hated Big Mullen, but she wouldn't want to see him dangling, she wouldn't want to see the devil himself dangling. What was to be done? She put this to Sandy. 'What's to be done, boy?'

And now Sandy put to her the suggestion he had given to Stan. He said eagerly, 'Tom. We could tell Tom, he would do something. He'd get a gang on his side and go up there and haul Big Mullen and his lot out.'

His mother was shaking her head. 'You won't get Tom the day, not now,' she said slowly; 'he's gone into the hills for a meeting about a Union or somethin'. He . . . he wouldn't even tell me where.'

Sandy stared at her. Unconsciously she had told him a great deal with her words 'he wouldn't even tell ME where' and he felt that strange sadness flooding him again, even while he felt glad for her.

But that was beside the point. It was of no matter what his mother felt for Tom or Tom for her, there was just the possibility that they would be separated for ever after this night, for undoubtedly it would be the strikers as a whole who would get the blame for whatever happened at the Manor and he was knowledgeable enough to know that not only would the county be up in arms but also the whole nation. The poor man had few rights, but he'd have less in this county after this night.

She said now, 'Well, we just can't sit here and do nothing. If . . . if they're going to blow it up they've got gunpowder of sorts, haven't they?'

He nodded at her. 'Yes; what they use for blastin' the new faces down the pit, an' a bit makes a mighty bang an' brings a lot of stuff down; you have to scatter. But at the same time it would take a good few shots to blow up a house like the Manor.'

'D'you think they've got enough to do it?'

He nodded dolefully. 'They wouldn't try else.'

She was leaning towards him now. 'Gunpowder doesn't go off if it's wet, does it?'

'No.'

'Well, what about us trying to wet it?'

'Wet it?'

'Aye, there's the old gourd there, we could fill it full of water. I could go up with you to this place an' I could give a good account of meself with a stick.'

'Don't be daft, Ma.'

She was on her feet, her voice loud now. 'I'm not daft, lad. And let me tell you somethin'. It won't be the first time I've wielded a pick shank at a man's head; I was only fifteen when I was in the riots.' Her voice trailed away and she closed her eyes tight, and he stared at her for a moment. He had never heard before of her being in the riots. He said quietly, 'But it's an awful job gettin' up, you've got to scramble.'

'I can scramble, lad. Come on, get that gourd; we'll fill it at the stream on our way. But—' she paused and said now, 'Your hands, are they painful?' and he answered, 'They're all right.'

When they reached the foot of the bracken-covered hill he nodded to her to be quiet. He had told her what she had to do and, like Stan had done earlier in the day, she crawled after him up the steep hill in the shadow of the bracken; and when at last they came to the spot where Sandy and Stan had lain earlier, she pulled herself to his side and, their cheeks on the ground, they lay looking at each other with ears cocked, listening.

They must have lain like this for a full fifteen minutes, then Sandy raised his head and shook it slowly as if to say, there's no one there, but we'd better make sure, and she nodded to this. Then pulling the gourd gently towards her, for it was she who had insisted on dragging it up the hill, she got to her knees and made to rise, but Sandy's hand halted her. Taking the gourd from her he handed her the pick shank before he crawled forward as stealthily as he could towards the cave entrance. There, he paused for a moment and looked back at her, and she gave him a half smile as if to reassure him that she was with him all the way. But her idea at this moment seemed more improbable than ever to him, yet, as she said, it was the unlikely things that came off. Element of surprise, she said. If he could spot the charges all he had to do was to dash forward and throw the water over them. That was all, just dash forward. His thoughts were derisive now. All this would end in was a broken head and her likely tied up.

His head poked forward, he was on one knee ready to spring. But he didn't spring. As he stared through the dimness into the empty cave he slowly pulled himself through the opening and to his feet, and as he felt his mother rising from the earth at his side he let his gaze rest on her for a moment, then said, 'They've gone, all of them.'

He walked forward. The fire was almost dead; the only evidence of their presence was a number of empty bottles lying in the corner and some rabbit bones sticking out of the ash.

'They've been frightened off,' she said. 'Thank God. Thank God.' He felt her body slowly subsiding with her relief, but he couldn't share it. Knowing Big Mullen, he couldn't see him giving up, not at this stage. But they had certainly gone. However, they could be inside there. He looked towards the bed in the corner. The bracken was laid out neatly. No, if there was anybody down there the bracken wouldn't be like that unless they had left someone up above to straighten it and cover their tracks. He just couldn't understand it. Of one thing though he was certain, Big Mullen hadn't given up. He'd likely come back after the fair; and he said so, then added, 'Come on, let's get out of here.'

He dropped on to his hands and knees again and crawled out, his mother following, and when they were hidden in the bracken once more she said softly, 'You think they'll come back?'

'Aye, sure of it,' he said. . . .

Time passed and the light changed; the long twilight had begun. At one point Sandy whispered, 'You go on down.' And she whispered back, 'Don't be silly; you can't tackle them on your own.'

He knew this to be true, but he could see that she was cramped and tired, and her face looked drawn.

When the light deepened still further he turned to her and said, 'Something must have happened, he wouldn't be at the fair at this time. It doesn't look as if they're comin' back here after all. . . . Come on, let's go down.' And thankfully she obeyed him.

But they had no sooner rounded the mound and

135

slithered to the bottom of the hill than Sandy gripped her arm, warning her to lie still for his ears had picked up the sound of running steps. When he heard the steps coming directly towards him he reached out and grabbed the pick shank from her, then raising his head slightly he glimpsed the runner, and the next minute he was on his feet, crying, 'Oh! it's you, Stan.'

Stan stumbled forward and, looking his surprise as Norah Gillespie pulled herself up from the ground, said breathlessly, 'I ... I've been lookin' all over for you; never thought you'd be here 'cos I knew ... knew you were out with your mother—' he nodded deferentially to Norah Gillespie – 'Joe saw you. You'd better come back sharp; Old ... Old Mark's in your house.'

'What!'

Norah Gillespie stiffened at the idea of the dirty old wild man being in her house, as poor as it was, but Sandy's exclamation was bred of a different thought. 'Is ... is he all right?' he asked.

'I don't know. I don't know whether he's drunk or bad; he's been jabbering all the time, but he'll tell me nowt because, well because of me da. He wants to see you. ... Come on.'

They were running now, Norah Gillespie as swiftly as the boys, with her skirts held up to her knees.

'He'll likely be gone,' gasped Sandy as they came within sight of Ballast Row.

'I don't think so,' said Stan; 'he was all out; I think he'd been dodgin' them. His leg stump is torn and bleedin'.'

When they entered the house it was to see Old Mark lying full length on the clippie mat close to the fire as if begging warmth, yet the day was still hot. His eyes were closed, until Sandy knelt down beside him and said softly, 'Mark! Mark!' Then the old man's lids moved upwards in the deep hollows of hair and when he recognized Sandy's face his mouth began to work and he pulled himself on to his elbow and muttered, 'Lad! Lad!' Now he raised his eyes to where Norah Gillespie was standing looking down at him, and Sandy said, 'It's me ma, Mark, I told you of her. An', an' you know Stan. Stan's all right, Mark, he's ... he's not like his da.'

'N-o Mul-len's all right.'

'Stan is.' Sandy's voice was soft and reassuring, but Old Mark still shook his head. Then gripping Sandy's arm, he said, 'Bad business, boy, bad business. Gona blow it up, the house. Gona blow the house up.'

Sandy now supported the old man with his arm as he asked, 'When? When, Mark?'

'The night.'

'But ... but there's nobody there. We've just been up, me ma and me, to the cave.'

'They're there.' The old man nodded slowly. 'They're there, all right, lad, inside.'

'Inside?'

'Aye, three of them. They left one up top to see to me an' cover the traces, you know, me bed, straighten me bed. He lay on it and dropped asleep. Comfortable that bed comfortable.' The hair on his face rippled slightly, then he added, 'I got out. I had to crawl; they had smashed me crutch. Got a stick, but not much use. Looked for you, lad.'

'Yes, yes, you did.' Sandy patted the hooked hand that was raised to him. He had always been repulsed by the hook, but now he gripped it in tenderness and said slowly and quietly, 'Can you tell us what they're goin' to do, an' when?'

The old man nodded. Then taking his eyes from

Sandy's and looking at Stan he said, 'Sure about him?'

'Aye, I'll swear on it.'

'He told on me afore.'

'No, I didn't, never,' put in Stan now; 'I never told on you, Mark. The young 'uns, not me.'

'Well—' the old man swung his hairy head – 'somebody did, somebody did.'

'Tell us, Mark.' Sandy's tone was soft but urgent now. 'Tell us all you know.'

The old man leant towards him and, his hand gripping his wrist, the fingers pressing on the whip weal, he said, 'Soon as it's dark. It's all set, it's . . . it's right under the floor. Not near the fireplace, no. You know where I showed you, where the smell came up from the kitchen. Well round there, atween the kitchen ceiling and the floor under their dining room and their parlour, that's where it's set.'

'But they mightn't be in there,' Sandy put in now.

'Oh, they'll be in there all right. They've picked the night, party, big party the night, house full. If they're not in one place they'll be in t'other; even might be in the Hall holdin' their fine dances. Oh, Big Mullen's planned it for the right time.'

'But—' Sandy was shaking his head quickly now – 'they'll go up with it themselves.'

'Not them, lad, not them; they've brought the trail of powder right to the rock, you know, where the door is bunged up into the old workin's. They've planned everything to the minute. They'll light the fuse from there, an' by the time it reaches the House they'll be in the cave and away. It'll be dark and then they'll be in their beds with their women folk to swear that they've never been out of them.'

'But ... but me da went to the fair the day.' It was Stan's voice muttering now; and the old man looked at him again and said, 'Your da thinks of everythin', lad; he went to the fair and made himself seen at the fair, but he was back like a streak of lightnin', and he's been down there with the others doin' the job. An' you can take it from me it'll be done properly; there's no one can set a charge like John Felton. He's as good as his da afore him and I should know 'cos I worked with him for years.'

Ten

Sandy let the old man lie back now. Standing up, h
looked from his mother to Stan, then to the clock o
the mantelpiece. But he had to go towards it to mak
out the time. It said twelve minutes to nine. He turne
now, his breathing rapid as if he was still running, an
said, 'It's just over an hour afore dark. Look, we've go
to do something.' He watched his mother clasp her hand
and walk round the table, saying as she went, 'If onl
there was somebody, somebody we could go to; if onl
Tom was here.' She stopped. 'He should be back now
he might be home now. Sandy, go on, run into Hebburn
You know where he lives, tell him.'

'No, Ma, no.' He shook his head rapidly. 'By the tim
I got there and he got back, half-an-hour would be gon
an' if we managed to fight our way into the cave o
into the passage, it wouldn't be any use then; they coul
set the fuse and fight us off, it's so narrow. It's got to b
from the other way, from the Manor.'

'But you've tried that way, boy.'

'Not enough, not enough,' he said now. 'I've got t
get in; I will get in.'

'It's over four miles, you'll never make it.'

'I will, Ma, I will.'

'Where are you goin'? What are you gona do?' Sh
came to the door with him and grabbed his arm; an

he turned to her but looked towards Stan, saying, 'You dash into Hebburn, Stan. You know Quarry Hill?' He didn't wait for Stan to answer. 'Forty-two, number forty-two, that's where Tom lives. Fetch him, and any others you can get. Take them to the cave; it's a chance, if I don't get through, well they might. . . just.'

'But how are you going to get there in time, let alone get in?' His mother was shaking his arm.

'On The Nipper, Ma. The Nipper.' He pushed his face towards her and said, 'On the dratted Galloway.' Then he was off, out of the door racing towards the pit and the field behind it. And his mind too raced as he ran. How long would it take The Nipper to do the four miles to the Manor? Half-an-hour? No, he was fresh, he could do it in less. But first he had to get to him. Then when he reached the Manor he had to get in. Aye, that was going to be the hardest part, getting in. But as his dad used to say, 'Never worry how you're going to feel at the end of the day, if you do you'll be tired afore you start. One step at a time, lad; one step at a time.'

In the soft glow of the twilight he saw the field ahead and The Nipper standing alone away from the rest, his head over the rough gate as if he was waiting for him.

He leant on the gate for a moment panting while The Nipper tossed his head and neighed softly; then he muttered between gasps, 'Right, lad. Right, lad. You're going to have the fastest gallop of your life.' Quickly unbarring the gate, he led The Nipper through, then having put the bar in place again he grasped the pony's mane and swung himself up on to his back. He had no need to give any order, the slightest pressure of his heels and they were off; and not forgetting for a moment the reason for his errand, the joy pulsing through The Nipper's body was transferred to his own, and they became one again.

Near the cross-roads they startled a group of people returning from the fair. They were evidently townspeople making their way back to Jarrow and Hebburn and both men and women seemed the worse for drink. They squealed and yelled and jumped into the ditch on one side or up the bank on the other as he rode through them, and their laughter and their curses followed him.

The shortest route, he knew, would be by the toll gate, then across the fells. But he didn't want to be held up at the toll gate; the old woman there took her time, she was a cranky old thing. No, he'd have to add another half-a-mile to his journey, which would likely make it shorter in the long run.

His mind still planning, he thought, I'll go through that wood and over the burn. But again he discarded the idea. The light would be fading fast when he got to the wood and there was always the danger of those vicious traps; he couldn't let The Nipper run that risk. No, it would have to be the twisting bridle path until he came to the open land; he considered that narrow brush-bordered way couldn't be any worse than the pot-holed rutted main road. It was well for them both that The Nipper was sure-footed.

And now he was turning off the road and galloping The Nipper into what looked like an impregnable thicket. He winced as the brambles tore at his bare legs, and in places he had to bury his face in The Nipper's mane to avoid being caught up in overhanging branches. But all the while he encouraged the pony. 'It's all right, lad, you're doing fine. Keep at it, keep at it. That's a lad.'

In the open once more the fell land stretched before them, two miles across this, and then a mile up the road past the farm and along by the wall he'd be at the place where he had entered the grounds earlier in the day.

He had never known The Nipper go so fast, it was as if he, too, realized the urgency of the situation. He had never known a twilight fall into night so fast either, for it was almost dark now. There seemed to be no air, the night was heavy and clammy, portending rain. He felt the sweat from The Nipper mingling with his own, but he knew that more than half his own sweat was caused by fear.

They were now clear of the fells and on the roadway and The Nipper was still galloping gallantly, his hoofs beating rhythmically. The sound filled Sandy's ears, vibrated through his head and seemed to set the pace to his breathing.

They passed the farm. It was no use stopping here, the time now was too short for that. Then they came to the wall from which he had seen the young lady in the gig, and for the first time The Nipper came to a halt. The Nipper wasn't a jumper; he had cleared the four-foot ditch time and time again in Farmer Blyth's field but a four-foot wall was a different thing altogether. He stood, his head bobbing and his nostrils sending forth a white vapour like steam.

Aw no; they weren't going to be baulked now. He hadn't thought of this. The house was a good mile away; it was no good trying to run there. He looked behind him. A ditch bordered the other side of the road, but a little way to the right was an entrance to a gateless field. That was it, it'd give him a long run.

In the field he patted The Nipper's neck, then whispered, 'Take it, boy, take it. Ready? Come on now.' With a sharp pressure of his knees, he drove The Nipper at the wall, and The Nipper galloped towards it, then came to a skidding stop, his four feet splayed, and Sandy just saved himself from going over his head and landing on the top of the wall.

Straightening himself again he turned The Nipper back into the field, and once again, bending low, he patted him and said, 'Now this time, lad, take it, take it.' Again he pressed his knees into the flanks, and again The Nipper charged at the wall, and Sandy almost laughed aloud as he felt his body rise in the air, The Nipper still between his legs. There was the sound of hooves hitting the top of the wall. The Nipper stumbled but righted himself sharply again. They were over and galloping across the field towards the broken wall.

Now the pony was in his stride again and they streaked across the parkland where, in the distance, like a thousand stars coming out in the night sky, the lights from the house shone, and as Sandy raced towards them he felt as if he was flying into heaven itself.

But now the nearer they came to the house the slower became their progress, for they were in gardens with ornamental trees all around, some, cut out like great beasts, merged with the fast approaching darkness and had a terrifying appearance. Now they were threading their way through a rose garden and the perfume came to him in waves and he thought he had never smelt anything like it in his life. On, on, he urged The Nipper until they were clear of the gardens, and there before him stretched a great lawn, and above it was perched the House. Across the lawn, up four shallow steps, and on to a wide drive, and now he pulled The Nipper to a stop and as the pony snorted loudly and eased its lungs, he patted it soothingly and said, 'Good lad. Clever lad,' while he gazed about him.

The strange thing was he couldn't see a human being, yet the whole drive and as far as he could see into the stable yard held carriages and coaches, all with their shafts at an angle resting on the ground, which told him that the visitors inside the house had been there some time, for their horses had been stabled.

Sliding stiffly from The Nipper's back, he then led him between two of the carriages. He reached up and pulled a strap from the high seat of one of them and, having first put it round The Nipper's neck, attached it to the handle of the door; then saying hastily, 'Stay now. Stay. I'll be back,' he dodged between the rest of the lifeless carriages and made for the front steps of the House.

He realized now why there was no one about, for at the Harvest Supper Farmer Blyth's yard had also looked like this, only in a less fine way and with fewer carriages. Once the horses were seen to, everybody went to eat in the barn; later, the farm hands went into the stables and had their own jollification, while the farmer and his personal friends had theirs in the house. This was what was happening here only on a grand scale, and he was lucky it was so, for he considered even one coachman would have been a tough nut to crack.

He was halfway up the steps when he stopped. The doors of the house were wide open and he was looking on to a scene the like of which he had never even dreamed about. He had never imagined there was so much colour in the world. He had seen the fells covered with heather; he had seen woods in snow drifts of wood anemones; and he had seen banks drifting with bluebells like sea waves; but all that was dull to what he was looking on now. There were ladies dressed in gold, which colour seemed brighter than the sun, and green velvets that put young grass to shame; there were violets and soft pinks that you sometimes glimpsed streaking a wet sky when the sun came out after a storm; and all about there were shining, laughing faces.

Slowly he mounted another two steps and saw the ladies moving as if in procession across the hallway to a far door, and their laughter and voices came to him like tinkling music.

Two lackeys dressed handsomely in blue and grey cord suits with white stockings passed across his eye level. One man's stockings, he saw, had yellow garters. He rose another slow step for his amazement had for the moment shut down all thought in his mind except that for the scene on which he was looking. He was in the outer hall now and walking slowly towards the main door, and the grandeur of the hall lifted his eyes upwards to the glistening candelabra, where hundreds of candles flickered, then swiftly down to a door to the right of him from which were emerging two more lackeys bearing great silver trays on which were the remains of food.

He had actually taken four steps into the hall before anyone saw him, and then it was one of the servants who were carrying the trays, and the tray shook in the man's hand as he cried to the man with the gold coloured gaiters, 'Mr Banner! Mr Banner! Look!' When the butler turned and saw Sandy his astonishment stretched his face, then swelled his body with indignation, which checked his speech for a moment. But now, advancing on Sandy, his voice low and threatening, he muttered, 'How did you get in here? Get out! Out this instant! Portman!' He turned to a footman. 'Get this creature. . . .'

His words were now cut off by Sandy, who seeming to come alive again to the urgency of his presence here yelled at the top of his voice, 'I'll not! I'll not! I must see the master. You're in danger. You're all in danger. You're going to be blown up . . . BLOWN UP.'

There were hands on him now, seemingly dozens of hands. He was being borne towards the door, and he struggled and kicked and tore at the hands while he yelled, 'I tell you, they're goin' to blow the house up, the miners. The miners, they're going to blow the house up.'

The word miners seemed to re-echo round the hall and it brought to a stop the remainder of the ladies who were going into the drawing-room. It brought the dining-room door bursting open and a tall figure came striding out, demanding in outraged tones, 'What is this! What is this ! Banner! What is the meaning of this?'

The butler, panting and standing aside, straightened his coat while pointing to his underlings who were holding Sandy as if he were a wild bull, and he said, 'It's regrettable, Sir, it's regrettable. . . .'

The tall man glared at Sandy and ground out through clenched teeth, 'Get rid of him immediately.'

'Sir! Sir! They're goin' to blow your house up. There's not much time, you'll all be killed. Sir! Sir!'

'Shut up you!' There was a hand clapped across his mouth, and he was forced backwards and he felt himself being dragged from the room, his bare heels pulling up rugs as he went, when the progress was suddenly halted by a voice thundering, 'Stay! Stay!'

Now he found himself being pushed upwards on to his feet again but with his head held painfully back as one of the lackeys gripped his hair. He gazed up at the face above him and in spite of the excruciating pain in his neck he appealed to it, 'Please. Please, Sir, believe me. They're goin' to blow up the house. It . . . it could happen any minute; they're underneath—' he tried to indicate the floor – 'with gunpowder. I, I tried to tell you afore. . . .'

Now there was another face looking at him. This he recognized as the girl's who had used her whip on him, and, her voice low, she said, 'Father, this...this is the boy I told you about, who stopped the gig; he...he was trying to tell me something then. I...I didn't understand what he said.'

'Let him go!' On the command, Sandy was free and standing upright, and he stood for a moment rubbing his neck and looking at the great circle of faces about him; then with a sudden movement he stepped close to the tall man and his words tumbled over each other as he said, 'Please, Sir, please, clear the house. I don't know how much time you've got, they're...they're goin' to do it when it's dark. It—' he flung his hand back towards the open door – 'it's almost that now. Another ten minutes, fifteen. Please, please Sir, believe me.'

'Follow me!' The tall man now hurried through the throng of men surrounding the dining-room door; then, stopping abruptly, he called the butler to him and said quietly, 'Just in case, be prepared to get the ladies out on to the lawn.' He then went further into the dining-room, pushing Sandy before him now, the men following.

The room seemed full of men, ten or more, handsomely dressed, forbidding men, masters all. But Sandy didn't look at them. Quickly he scanned the large room. There was the fireplace. He dodged past the men and ran towards it, and looked from one side of the great wooden frame to the other, where on each side panel a large boar's head was carved; and now turning to the master of the house, he cried, 'It's...it's behind here, Sir, the...the secret room.'

'Secret room? What are you talking about, boy?'

'There's a secret room behind here, Sir, and it runs over the kitchen and partly under here—' he pointed to the floor – 'and your parlour.'

'Secret room?' There was murmuring among the men,

and one coming forward, said, 'There is a secret room here, William,' and Sir William Combe Stockwell turned on him abruptly, saying, 'That was blocked up years ago, filled in, before our time here. The entrance was above a cupboard in the kitchen quarters. It's roofed in with solid stone – it's there for you to see – and I understood the place itself was filled in. I've never heard of any other secret room.'

'Sir! Sir! I can show you, the boar's head.'

'The boar's head?'

'Yes, Sir, up the nose. That's where the spring is.' Sandy looked from one side to the other, stumped now, for the two heads were exactly alike. But he dashed to the right side one first and, thrusting his fingers up the boar's nostrils, he pressed and looked upwards to see if the panel moved. But nothing happened. When he turned they were all staring at him. He now ran to the other side of the fireplace, almost, in his haste, tripping over the huge iron fire dogs that held the dead logs of wood. Now he was pressing his fingers up these two nostrils, and he almost laughed with sheer relief and nervousness as he felt the springs give; then before his eyes the panel began to move.

They were all about him, almost smothering him as they stared into the darkness beyond, but no one said a word for a moment until Sir William startled them all by crying to the man next to him, 'Get them out, Braintree! Everybody, everybody. Quickly!'

'You mean clear the whole house?'

'Yes, yes; if the boy's right about this he could be right about the rest. . . . get them out.'

There was a scampering now towards the door, not only by Mr Braintree but also by most of the rest of the company. Only three men stayed besides Sir William, and he turned to the first one and said, 'Bring the candelabra, Conisbie.' He pointed to the table.

At this stage the young girl came rushing up the room, crying, 'Father! Father!' and he shouted at her angrily, 'Get away, child! Take your mama and get out.'

'But Father. . . .'

'Get out! Do as you're bid, instantly!'

There was great commotion coming from the hall now. No longer were the voices filled with laughter like tinkling music, there were now only squeals and cries of alarm.

As one of the men swiftly led the young girl from the room the master called a servant to him and said something about a gun. Seconds later the servant came running and handed his master a pistol.

The man called Conisbie had two candelabra in his hands now, each holding six candles, and Sir William, taking one from him, held it above his head and bent forward to peer into the darkness beyond. Then turning his head towards Sandy he said sharply, 'Get inside!' and Sandy, after swallowing his spittle, went forward into the room and Sir William followed him. After them came the man called Braintree and another whom the master addressed as Farrington.

The room was illuminated now and Sandy saw it in its entirety for the first time.

'Well, this is something.' It was Farrington speaking. 'Who would have thought of this? You know I . . . I've heard tell of a passage. . . .'

Sir William's voice cut him short now, saying, 'More of that later. Where are the explosives, boy?'

'They must be under there, Sir.' He was pointing to the hole that led under the floors when Mr Braintree cried, 'Look, there!' and whipping the candelabrum from Mr Conisbie's hand and going further into the room he bent down, and the light from the candles revealed three uneven lines of gunpowder leading to the hole that Sandy had indicated.

'My God!' It was a concerted exclamation from the men.

'God in heaven!'

'What's to be done?'

The voices were all around; they seemed for the moment to be unaware of the obvious, that in breaking the trail of gunpowder they would eliminate the danger. It had also escaped Sandy for the moment, until, looking up the passage that led from the room, he saw in the far distance a creeping light. His voice breaking on a high note, he cried, 'They've . . . they've set it, the fuse. Scatter the powder!' He was now rubbing his feet over the lines. Then, whipping off his coat, he ran from them and along the passage and threw it over the fast creeping flames, beating at it with his hands. Then there were others doing the same. The passage seemed packed to suffocation with the four of them, and one man kept repeating all the time, 'My God! My God! What an escape.'

When the fuses were extinguished, Sir William, turning to Sandy and his voice laden with awe, said 'Boy, what we owe you!' The others murmured, 'Indeed! Indeed!'

There was silence in the passage for a moment, until one of the men exclaimed, 'They can't be far, the rascals can't be far.'

'Come on, let's get them!' It was the voice of Mr Farrington, and Sandy looked at the man. He was young, younger than Tom Fitzsimmons; he was beautifully dressed, almost foppishly so, but there was no foppishness about his manner, and Sir William echoed him, saying, 'Yes, yes. Lead the way, boy. Lead the way.'

But Sandy remained still. The danger was over, nobody was to be killed, and in this moment he did not want Big Mullen and his pals to be caught for that would mean the gibbet for them. He thought of Stan. Whatever happened to Big Mullen would affect Stan. He tried to stall any move along the passage by saying 'Well, it's over now, Sir, you're all safe.'

'It isn't over, boy.' The face of the master looked stern again. 'It'll never be over while there are villains like this at large. Those men knew what they were doing; they meant to blow up my house, and but for you, boy, they would have achieved their evil purpose. Do you know how many people were in this house tonight? Twenty-six guests besides the servants. Just think, boy, just think. And now, as you seem to be acquainted with this route, lead the way.'

There was nothing for it but to go forward. But just before they started Sir William said, 'Go back, Braintree, will you and tell them it's all right, the danger's over. And send Portman and Fawcett down, and one or two of the others. Tell them to hurry along after us. Who knows, we may need assistance.'

When they reached the crevasse in the rock Sandy looked back. There were still only two men besides the master following, the one called Farrington, and the other, Conisbie. In the ordinary way he knew they wouldn't have a chance against Big Mullen, John Felton and the other two, but the master had a pistol. Yet there was nothing for it, he had to go on. But no; he stayed their progress for a few minutes when, a thought coming into his head, he stopped abruptly and said, more to himself than to them, 'The Nipper, he's back there.'

'The who?'

'The Nipper, the pony that I came on.'

'Oh.' Sir William tossed his head impatiently. 'He'll be all right, boy.'

'But Sir, he doesn't like to be handled by anybody else but me.'

'Boy!' The master was trying to keep the impatience from his voice. 'We have more important things to think about at the present moment than your pony. Go on, lead the way.'

They passed through the crevasse and continued along the passage, but although they stopped and listened several times there was no sound of anyone running ahead, only the silence of their own breathing. That was until they came near the end of the passage and in sight of the trap door. Sandy lifted up his hand, then pointed, and when the candelabrum was held high it shone on the sloping slab, and from beyond this there came the sound of murmuring voices.

Sandy, reluctantly, was about to stand on the stones and reach upwards when Sir William put out his hand and pressed him aside, and he himself climbed the stones and slowly put his head through the trap door. Then, his movements surprisingly agile for so big a man, Sandy saw him swing himself upwards and through the hole and heard his voice, crying, 'Hold! Make a move any of you and I'll blow your brains out.'

Sandy was the last to scramble upwards; he didn't hurry his entry for he didn't want to face Big Mullen and his pals. They were bad men, he knew they were bad men; still, he was reluctant to prove to them that he was the means of sending them to the gibbet.

Pulling himself up from the floor he stood with his head bowed; then it jerked up so rapidly that he felt a painful kink in his neck for there, kneeling on the floor by Tom Fitzsimmons's side, was his mother, and a little way off, looking down on the prostrate form of Big Mullen, was Stan.

He pushed past the master of the Manor and the other two men and shouting, 'Ma! Ma!' He dropped on to his knees beside her, and she put her arms around him as she gabbled, 'Oh, boy! Boy. Oh, thank God!'

'What happened, Ma? What happened?'

'We were too late, though we met Tom here on the road,' she said. 'He was coming to see us. We came straight on up. They were just coming out. Tom fought with Big Mullen. One of the others had a gun. He went to shoot Tom. The bullet grazed his shoulder—' She pointed down to Tom's blood-soaked shirt, and added softly – then caught Big Mullen, full on.'

Sandy looked at Stan. His head was bowed on his chest as he looked down on the contorted but very still form.

The three men from the Manor moved forward now and Sandy, getting to his feet, said, 'This is my mother, Sir, and our friend, Mr Fitzsimmons. An' my pal.' He pointed towards Stan. 'We arranged that they should try to stop them this way if . . . if I failed to get into your house.'

'What is the name of that man?' Sir William Stockwell asked now, pointing down to the figure of Big Mullen, and before Sandy could say anything Stan lifted his stiff white face towards the master and said bitterly, 'Mullen; and he's me father.'

The master was now looking from Stan to Sandy, and he said, 'You say this boy is a friend of yours?'

'Yes Sir. I . . . I can explain it, Sir. He . . . he tried to stop his da. If it hadn't been for him I . . . I would never have reached your house the night.' This wasn't exactly true but in this moment Sandy knew he had to place Stan in good stead with the owner of the mine. Stan was a pitman too and it would be hard for anyone to believe that a boy would go against his father, especially a man like Big Mullen.

'There's more to this than meets the eye.' Sir William turned now and, thrusting his pistol into the back pocket of his tail coat, he said, 'And this man?'

Tom was now struggling to his feet. He was dazed, not so much from the skin wound, but from a blow on the head he had received from Mike Casey when he was struggling with Big Mullen. He held his head now as he said slowly, 'What the boy says is true, Sir.'

'Who are you?'

Tom looked at his master, for indeed Sir William Combe Stockwell was his real master, and he said, 'A miner . . . in your pit. Perhaps you don't know it, Sir, but the men are on strike at the moment.'

In the flickering candlelight the two men of a like height surveyed each other, the privileged and the under-privileged, and the master, his voice cold and haughty, said, 'I am well aware that there is a strike at my mine. But what do you think you will achieve by blowing up my house and all the people in it?'

'Neither I, nor the men that are with me, had any intention of committing such a crime.'

Sir William nodded slowly. 'Ah! You have men then, you are the leader of the rebel faction?'

'I speak for a section of the men, Sir; that section who just want rights, who want to negotiate. Big Mullen there—' he pointed down to the floor – 'he led another faction, much smaller, who considered it was useless to try to talk to—' he paused – 'to the owners. They wanted action.'

They stared at each other for a moment longer, then Sir William turned his eyes away and, looking down at the twisted form on the ground, said, 'Is he dead?'

'Aye, he's dead.' It was Stan speaking again.

'Well, that's saved him the gallows, hasn't it?' On this the master turned abruptly about, saying, 'Come back with me, all of you.'

'Me an' all?' It was a soft question from Norah Gillespie. And they all looked in her direction and the master said, 'Yes, you and all.'

Sandy felt his jaws tighten at the way his mother was being addressed, but they slackened somewhat when Mr Conisbie and Mr Farrington helped both her and Tom down through the trap door.

He himself stood at the top of the door about to drop down into the hole when he looked to where Stan was standing still gazing at his father, and he ran back to him and grabbed his arm, saying, 'Come on, Stan. Come on.'

'No, I'm not goin'.' The voice was gruff.

'Look.' Sandy whispered now. 'You can do nothing here, it's over, finished. You . . . you've got to clear yourself. If you don't come they might try to tack something on to you. Come on, man. You can come back later for him.'

Stan paused for a moment; then reluctantly he allowed himself to be led to the trap door, and Sandy said, 'Just sit down and let yourself go.'

When they were all in the passage they moved in single file, Sandy bringing up the rear with Stan before him; in front, Tom and his mother.

When at last they reached the secret room behind the panel there were a number of people busying about, and a man was saying to Sir William, 'Look at this lot, William. Three sets at different points. My God! just think of what it could have done.' He pointed to the three groups of charges, about thirty pieces in all, and he said in awe,

'It's an arsenal. The whole place would have gone up.' There was silence for a moment; then Sir William let out an audible breath and said, 'Yes, the whole place could have gone up. Come on, let's get out of here.'

When Sandy passed through the narrow aperture into the dining-room he saw it was crowded with people, not only with gentlemen but with ladies too now, and the sight of the women was definitely displeasing to Sir William for he was saying tersely, 'Now didn't I send to tell you it was all right? You can adjourn to the drawing room, ladies.'

'Oh, William, William.' A plump lady was hanging on to his arm. 'Is it true? Were we going to be blown up? Those wicked men. Those wicked, wicked men.'

'Calm yourself, Amelia. See to your mama, Anna.' He motioned with a gesture towards his daughter; then turning to the butler, he said, 'Bring the decanters, Banner.' And when the butler had brought the decanters and glasses from the sideboard to the table Sir William turned and, looking towards Sandy, where he stood next to his mother, with Stan on the other side of him and Tom Fitzsimmons behind him, he moved towards them and said courteously, 'Be seated.' At the same time a wave of his hand brought the servants scurrying forward with four chairs.

After they had sat down silently and self-consciously, Sir William poured out four glasses of wine and he himself handed them, one to each, and they thanked him in their different ways. But they didn't put the wine to their lips until all the men in the room had glasses in their hands. Then Sir William, raising his own glass and looking at Sandy, said, 'Our thanks to you, boy. Our grateful thanks.' And on this there came a chorus of voices from the men, 'Indeed! Indeed, our grateful thanks.' This went on for some seconds, and then they all drank and Sandy, his face red and his hands sweating, took his first sip of real wine and thought he had never tasted anything like it in his life, as indeed he hadn't.

Sir William now addressed him, saying, 'Now boy, tell us from the beginning about this whole episode.' And on this command Sandy looked apprehensively from his mother to Stan, and then to Tom. But his mother remained quiet, as did Stan. It was Tom who said, 'The damage is done now, boy, tell what you know.'

And so, haltingly but briefly, he told of the meeting with Mad Mark, and of Big Mullen's methods in trying to get the old man to talk. He told of Stan's opposition to his father. He stressed this part of his story, and when he came to the strike he let his imagination run rife about Tom's eloquence and his handling of the men; lastly he spoke of The Nipper, the pit pony, and immediately he mentioned his name he remembered that The Nipper was still tethered to a coach, and he got to his feet quickly and said, 'Sir! Sir! could I, please, see to him? He'll be missing me.'

'Oh,' said Sir William airily now; 'I should think he's been attended to.' He looked round the room, and one of the lackeys coming deferentially towards him, said, 'The pony has been taken to the stables, Sir.'

'There, does that ease your mind?'

'Yes, Sir.' Sandy sat slowly down again.

'Well now, boy.' Sir William also seated himself, as did most of the ladies around the dining table, and Sir William waited for their rustling and fluttering to stop before he went on, 'I am deeply aware at this moment that I not only owe you my life, and that of my family, but also the lives of all my guests.' He looked around the company and there were loud cries of 'Hear! hear! True, true.

Indeed, indeed.' And then he went on, 'And I for one would like to repay that debt as much as lies in my power.... Is there anything you want, boy?'

Was there anything he wanted? If he lived to be a hundred he never expected anyone to say that to him. Was there anything he wanted? He wanted.... What did he want? Why the only thing he wanted was to own The Nipper and ... and his mother to have a nice house and ... and of course Stan, he wanted Stan to be happy, and he wanted Tom to have a fair deal, and Tom having a fair deal would mean the rest having a fair deal, and he wanted, oh, he wanted to work on a farm again.

WHAT WAS THE MATTER WITH HIM? Had he gone barmy? The master had just asked him what he wanted, and he thought he only wanted to own The Nipper, but here he was wanting the world.

They were all looking at him. All these eyes were on him. The room was full of eyes and smiling faces. He heard someone laugh and say, 'He's tongue-tied.' Then came the sound of coins hitting a plate and he turned his eyes, with those of the rest, to a man standing behind a lady seated at the top of the table. It was the man Sir William had called Conisbie and Conisbie was saying, 'There, boy, that's my contribution,' and he was about to hand the plate to the next man when Sir William's voice checked him saying in a stiff tone, 'Thank you, Conisbie, but this is primarily my debt; allow me to discharge it.' He again turned to Sandy and said, 'Well boy, tell me what you wish for yourself and if it lies within my power it shall be granted.'

Sandy looked back into the eyes of the mine owner and it was in this moment that he really became a man, for he knew that such a space in time, such an opportunity would never come his way again. In this moment he could ask things of the Lord of the Manor that good honest men would never dare to voice for a generation or more. This was a God-given moment, it was a moment that happened to few, but it was happening to him and he must make use of it. He gulped on his spittle, then said in a steady voice, 'I would like six ponies, Sir.'

The room was quiet. Sir William screwed up his eyes and looked down on the boy. Then his gaze slanted to the side where the eyes of his friends were on him, sporting men to the last one, lovers of horses, betting men. They all knew what value he put on his stables and they knew that he had but five young promising colts. He mouthed 'Six ponies?' before he actually spoke the words, and the way he said them told Sandy that his request had not met with approval, far from it, so he put in hastily, 'There's four of them for the knacker's yard, Sir. The Nipper, him outside—' he jerked his head back – 'he's the only decent one, the others are past it.'

Sandy watched Sir William's face stretch now, the lips pull away from the nose, to be drawn in for a moment between the teeth; he watched the head nod and the voice that came to him held deep amusement as he said, 'Six of my pit ponies?'

'Yes, Sir.'

A murmur of merriment spread around the room; then it died away as Sir William said in some bewilderment, 'But what do you intend to do with six ponies, four of which are ... past it?'

'Let them stay up top, Sir, for the rest of their days, in a field.'

There was a heavy silence on the room now. It was broken by a rustling and murmuring from the ladies as they turned to each other. Now Sir William was speaking again. 'And you would want some place to keep them – a field with water – and shelter?'

Their eyes were still holding. 'Yes, Sir.'

'How do you intend to feed them?' There was a quirk to Sir William's lips now.

Sandy could make no reply, and at this moment he became consciously aware of his mother, he could even hear her thinking, Six dratted ponies now. OH NO!

'Count me responsible for their feed.'

The voice came from the middle of the table and all eyes were turned on the man who had spoken them, and to him Sir William addressed himself, and rather coldly, saying, 'Thank you, Campbell, but as I've already said, and as you all know—' his eyes swept the table – 'I prefer to discharge my own debts.' He turned slowly to Sandy again, adding, 'So, boy, you have six ponies, a field, and feed for them as long as they require it. Does that satisfy you?'

'Yes, Sir.'

Sir William narrowed his eyes. 'You don't sound over sure. What is it? Speak up. Is there something else you wish for?'

'Yes, Sir. Two, two things more, Sir.' He kept his gaze steady although there was a queasy feeling in his stomach as if he could be sick. He would have to say what he had to say and get it over with, and quick. He now glanced towards Stan, for the first of these two requests was for him as well as himself. Stan was his mate, his marrer, and he knew he would never enjoy his good luck if Stan had bad. He said quickly, 'I want a job on a farm, Sir, along with me mate here, Stan.'

'Oh!' Sir William pursed his lips. 'Well, that I'm sure can be arranged. You would like it to be on my farm, I suppose?'

'Yes, Sir.'

'Is that one, or both of your requests?'

'Just one, Sir.'

'Well.' Sir William smiled. 'Let us have the last one.'

Sandy bit on his lip, gulped deep in his throat, then said quietly, 'The night's work, Sir, came about because the miners are dissatisfied.' He paused, and as he did so he realized that this one sentence had changed the atmosphere in the room, especially had it stiffened the countenance of the man before him. Nevertheless, he went on, because he knew that what he had to say now was more important than anything he had said before, more important than him having The Nipper in the open again, more important than working on the land, and this was the moment to say it, tomorrow would be too late for this man would never be in the same mood again, but any promise extracted from him now he would honour. Appealing straight to Sir William as the employer of the miners, he said, 'You have some good men in your mine, Sir, good workers, but they don't always get fair play an' they cannot have things put to rights 'cos they cannot talk to you. Tom, here,' he turned and looked at Tom who was staring fixedly at him, pride and encouragement in his eyes – 'Tom here has asked time and time again if it would be possible to have a word with you, to put the men's case afore you. It's no good puttin' it to the butties or the keekers, and the manager has a one-sided view, Sir. That's natural, 'cos he's thinkin' of you all the time. So Tom thought that if he could approach you face to face like and have a quiet talk, perhaps somethin' could be done. That's what he's wanted to do all along. That's what he tried to get Big Mullen to see, but . . . but he and his lot wouldn't have any of it. That's—' He gulped again. 'That's me last request of you, Sir, that you let Tom talk to you, at your convenience like, I mean.'

A pin could have been heard to drop in the room. Although the ladies were unaware of the importance of this request, they gauged from the manner of their men-folk that it was out of the ordinary – something beyond the bounds accorded to the common man was being requested.

The men themselves waited, each in his own way wondering how Stockwell would meet this unusual challenge. They were all masters of men and some of them believed, and acted in accordance with, a certain theory that was rife at this period, that the only way to keep the poor from taking over was to keep them hungry. As to allowing a common miner to put his case before the owner, it was unheard of. But this night was a special night; each man fully realized he was alive only because this boy had saved him, and he had saved him because he was a boy of initiative and sharp wits. Now he was putting his sharp wits to the test, and against Stockwell, and they were wondering, each of them, how Stockwell would react. He was not looking at the boy now but at the man with the blood-stained shirt who had risen to his feet. He was a well set-up man, honest looking; it would be hard to place him as one of the rabble; there was a dignity about him.

Still the company waited. Then Sir William returned his gaze to the boy, and now the look in his eyes was hard. He was caught in a cleft stick. The request had staggered him. He had been shaken when the boy asked for the field, for it would take a two acre field to graze six ponies, and a field was land and you didn't give land to the common folk, not even a quarter acre in which to keep a pig, not if you were wise. But because of the debt of lives that had to be paid, he had proposed it, and covered his feelings with a smile because ponies without a field was like a boxer without a backer. But land was one thing, the running of his mine was another. His penetrating gaze went deep into the eyes before him. He saw fear in them, but surmounting it he saw courage, and something akin to envy stirred in him. Why couldn't he, with all his wealth, have had a son like this? This boy was sharp, intelligent; he was taking advantage of a situation, not cunningly but in the manner of a fencer looking for openings, parrying, then thrusting forward straight to the point. His face relaxed, his head went back and he let out a bellow of a laugh as he cried, 'Gentlemen! who says that one day we won't see our young benefactor gracing the High Court as an advocate?'

This sally was greeted with a great burst of laughter, and when it had died away, Sir William again looked at Sandy, who was red in the face now, and said, 'Very well, boy, your last wish is granted.' Then, his gaze on Tom, he added, not unkindly, 'Tomorrow at eleven o'clock await me here.'

'Thank you, Sir. Thank you indeed.'

'And now I think you'd better have that shoulder seen to.' He nodded towards the still bright blood oozing through the shirt. 'And I'm sure you could all do with something to eat before you return to your homes. Banner.' He did not look round but waved his hand towards himself, and the butler came hurrying forward, and still not looking at Banner, but letting his gaze rest on Norah Gillespie now, he said, 'See that they're well fed; then tell Hanson to get the luggage coach ready and see them home.' And now he addressed Norah, saying, 'You can be proud of your son, Ma'am.' And to this she answered with a quiet dignity, 'I always have been, Sir; he takes after his father.'

'Your husband; where does he work?'

'My husband is dead, Sir.'

'Oh . . . well, you will not want for protection as long as you have that young man by your side.'

Norah Gillespie glanced at Sandy. His face was scarlet and his head was bowed. He stayed like this for a moment. Then looking once more up at Sir William he said quietly and with deep sincerity, 'Sir, I thank you for your kindness to me and mine. I will always be your man, Sir, wherever I am.'

The two confronted each other, and again Sir William felt the pain of regret at not having a son such as this.

With a slight wave of his hand he dismissed them and they followed the butler through the smiling throng of people.

It was as Sandy reached the bottom of the table that he caught the gaze of the young lady on him, and he once more felt the curl of her whip around his wrist, and when she stepped towards him and said, 'I'm sorry for my attitude this afternoon,' for a moment he could find nothing to say. It was a different thing to talk back to a man, but this girl here was a lady, and she was bonny. Yet not as bonny as Katie. Wait till he told Katie about everything. And, wonder of wonders, he would be working on the farm with Katie. His heart gave a little bound. Then it was with not a little amazement that he heard himself saying, 'That's all right, Miss; you couldn't know. It was an accident, like.' And, his smile widening, he added, 'You have a fine pony, a grand stepper.'

He had spoken casually as if talking to an equal and not to the daughter of the Manor House. And he had moved on through the doorway and across the hall, and was going down a dim passage, when Norah Gillespie said with a touch of sharpness in her voice 'Fancy speaking like that to Miss! The night's business has gone to your head; you forgot yourself, son.'

He looked at her steadily, then whispered, 'I forget nowt, Ma.' Then he grinned widely at her, and as she drew her head back from him as if to get him into focus, she saw that her lad was indeed a man. And his next words seemed to prove it, for with his grin even wider he ended, 'An' you'd better set an extra place for breakfast for I'm bringing that dratted Nipper in for his feed!'